For five whole minutes, while she and Toby prolonged their goodnight, Fran didn't think about her boyfriend's brother. It was so sweet to be together like this, so amazing to hear Toby say "I love you" for the first time, so earthshaking to say it back.

But after Toby had sped off down the quiet street and she was alone in her house, Fran dropped down from cloud nine with a thump.

In her moonlit room, with Drea breathing softly in the far bed, Fran stood in front of the shadowy mirror and stared at her own reflection. "I'm in love with Toby," she whispered to the mirror. "I *am*." But then why was her heart pounding not from the memory of Toby's kisses, but at the thought that the next day she might run into Marshall at the Art Institute?

Is Marshall the guy for me, or is Toby? Fran wondered. She didn't know a lot about love, but she was sure about one thing: They couldn't *both* be.

Behind His Back

DIANE SCHWEMM

BANTAM BOOKS
NEW YORK · TORONTO · LONDON · SYDNEY · AUCKLAND

In memory of my dear friend Monica.
I'll miss you.

RL 6, age 12 and up

BEHIND HIS BACK
A Bantam Book / September 1999

Cover photography by Michael Segal.

Produced by 17th Street Productions,
a division of Daniel Weiss Associates, Inc.
33 West 17th Street, New York, NY 10011.

ISBN: 0-553-49291-8

Published simultaneously in the United States and Canada

Bantam Books are published by Bantam Books, a division of Random House, Inc. Its trademark, consisting of the words "Bantam Books" and the portrayal of a rooster, is Registered in U.S. Patent and Trademark Office and in other countries. Marca Registrada. Bantam Books, 1540 Broadway, New York, New York 10036.

PRINTED IN THE UNITED STATES OF AMERICA

OPM   0 9 8 7 6 5 4 3 2 1

One

"THEY'RE DRIVING ME *crazy*," sixteen-year-old Fran Delaney declared. "The twins knocked over the oil painting I had drying in the garage—the canvas was trashed! And then Drea wallpapered our whole room with posters of James Van Der Beek. I'm ready to move out and rent my own apartment, Caley. I'm serious!"

Instead of sympathizing with her, though, Fran's best friend burst out laughing.

"It's not funny," Fran insisted, but she smiled despite herself. She'd been totally frustrated a few minutes earlier, but now, walking with Caley to the bus stop on this sunny late June morning, Fran felt herself relaxing.

"You were an only child for too long, that's all," Caley said, pushing back a strand of her chin-length brown hair. "You'll get used to having stepsibs."

"I liked being an only child," Fran reminded

Caley. "I don't want to get used to anything else."

Caley lifted an eyebrow. "Like you have a choice?"

Fran sighed. Caley had an excellent point. Fran *didn't* have a choice. Her father, an art history professor at Northwestern University, in Evanston, Illinois, had remarried a month ago after having been a widower for ten years. And that was that. *Voilà,* instant stepfamily. Emma and her three kids had moved in with Max and Fran, and now every meal was a huge production, and Emma kept trying to give Fran "motherly" advice about how to spend her summer vacation, and instead of peace and quiet there was always some violent, deafening Nintendo game blasting out of the TV set.

"It's just that I was happy with how things were before he met Emma," Fran tried to explain, even though she knew it was hard for Caley, who had four sisters and brothers of her own, to understand. The southbound bus to Chicago rumbled up to the corner, and she and Caley climbed on. "I thought Dad was too."

The girls dropped into a couple of empty seats near the back just as the bus lurched forward again. "Your dad was alone for a long time," Caley pointed out. "Obviously he finally felt ready to share his life with someone."

A dismal feeling crept over Fran. Pulling her long blond hair over one shoulder to braid it, she looked out the bus window at the sailboats on Lake Michigan. Her mother had died when Fran was in kindergarten, but Fran still felt horribly sad whenever she thought of her.

"Dad wasn't alone," she said quietly. "He had me."

Caley squeezed her hand. "You know it's not the same thing, Franny. I mean, he and Emma dated for only a few months—it must have been love at first sight."

Fran turned back to her friend. "I know," she admitted, struggling to push that old empty, lonely feeling back down below the surface. "And I'm happy for Dad. I really am. But Emma's taken over everything. Dad doesn't have time for anybody else."

Caley studied Fran for a moment. Then she broke out into a mischievous smile. "Know what I think? You need a boyfriend."

"Oh, right," Fran groaned, laughing. "Like that's the answer to everything?"

Caley's smile broadened. "Of course it is. And speaking of which . . ." She lowered her voice a notch. "Check out the guy in the red shirt and baggy jeans who got on at the last stop. Four rows up, on the other side of the aisle."

Fran glanced over at the guy in the red shirt just to humor Caley. *Definitely not my type,* she thought. Guys with muscles like that never read books, much less went to museums. "He's okay," she told Caley.

Caley's brown eyes grew wide. "Just okay?"

"Just okay."

"You're crazy." Caley craned her neck to get a better view. "He's gorgeous. Come on, let's scoot up to those empty seats right in front of him."

"We don't even know him!"

"Duh." Caley rolled her eyes. "That's the point. We *get* to know him."

"You go ahead and scoot," Fran said, squirming with embarrassment at the thought of trying to pick up a random guy. "I'm staying here."

Caley crossed her arms over her chest. "Frances Delaney, you'll never have a boyfriend if you don't get a little bolder."

Fran had to smile. "Caley Ann Woods, *you* can be as bold as you want, but I am not going to put the moves on some guy I happen—I mean, *you* happen—to spot on the bus."

"No?" Caley replied. "And where do you think you're going to meet guys this summer? Working for old Professor Baird? Hey, maybe you could score a date with him!"

"Caley, please!" Fran laughed. "He's a hundred years old!"

Unlike Caley, Fran hadn't taken a summer job in which she could meet lots of guys. She'd signed on for a part-time job with Professor Baird (even though Emma had urged her to do something more "fun") because she hoped to learn a lot from him. He was a renowned art historian as well as one of her father's colleagues. Plus her hours were flexible, so she could spend plenty of time sketching at the Art Institute, which was where she was on her way to now.

"That still doesn't mean I have to hit on Red Shirt Guy," Fran said. "There's such a thing as standards, you know."

4

"And standards can be too high," Caley countered.

"Mine aren't," Fran insisted.

"Then how come you still haven't found a guy? Standards can get in the way of fun, Franny."

"Well, I'm not in any hurry," Fran told Caley, settling back into her seat.

The truth was, most of the guys Fran met were just so *ordinary*. The really good-looking guys always seemed conceited, and plain-looking guys were, well, plain. Some guys weren't smart enough to have interesting conversations with, and a lot of smart guys were annoying know-it-alls. And most guys didn't know the first thing about art—since that was Fran's passion, it was important to her that the guy she was with shared it.

"I think it's worth waiting for someone perfect," she continued. "My parents had an incredible relationship, you know? Dad told me once that they were soul mates." She shook her head, suddenly annoyed. "That's why I can't believe he married Emma. She's so different from him! I mean, he's so classy, and she practically lives in sweatpants."

"Yeah, but she's a literary critic," Caley said. "At least she's intellectual, right?"

"She studies romance novels," Fran argued. "It's not exactly Shakespeare."

"True," Caley said, nodding. "But don't think I missed your change of subject! Back to your dream guy, who has to be perfect. Define 'perfect.'"

It seemed obvious to Fran, but she ticked off a list anyway. "Intelligent. Artistic. Sensitive. Romantic—

the kind of guy who brings you flowers for no reason. Oh, and good-looking. With a great body."

Caley smirked. "Good luck!"

Fran twirled her braid around her finger. "Why? What do you mean?"

"No such guy exists. Trust me."

"Well, I think he does. Somewhere," Fran said.

"Yeah, well, all I'm saying is if you wait for a guy who fits *that* bill, you'll be waiting a long time."

Fran just shrugged in response. She and Caley would never agree on the best way to have a love life.

The bus reached downtown Chicago. "Time to hit the phones," Caley said as the bus stopped near the tall office building where she had a receptionist job for the summer. "Look," she whispered as she stood up. "Red Shirt's getting off here too!"

"It's your lucky day," Fran whispered back.

Smiling, Fran watched out the window as Caley stepped down to the curb. She could see her friend say something to the guy in the red shirt. He checked his watch, and they exchanged a couple of words and smiles before the guy strode off.

Caley looked back to the bus. Lifting her left hand, Caley wiggled her ring finger. "Married!" she mimed to Fran with a tragic expression. "Can you believe it?"

Fran laughed to herself as the bus rolled off. *Married!* she thought, surprised. *That means the guy has to be at least . . . twenty or something.*

Fran shook her head. *Leave it to Caley,* she thought. Still, she knew her friend wasn't overly crushed. In a minute or two she'd find another guy to flirt with. Caley was never one to let herself get lonely for a guy.

Unlike Fran.

Fran sat up straighter in her seat at this thought. *Could Caley be right?* she wondered. *Am I lonely?*

Then she shook her head, forcing herself to snap out of it. How could she possibly be lonely when she had to share a house with Emma, Douglas, William, and Drea?

An hour later Fran was sitting on a bench in one of the Art Institute of Chicago's airy, sunlit galleries, doing a charcoal study of a Degas ballet picture. The museum was her favorite place in the world, and sketching there was her favorite activity. This summer she planned to spend as much time at the Art Institute as possible.

Usually she didn't pay much heed to the guided tours moving through the galleries. She'd been coming to the museum with her dad once or twice a month ever since she could walk and talk—she knew all there was to know about the Art Institute's collection. But that day a group gathering near *Ballet at the Paris Opera* caught her attention.

Something about this tour group was different.

"One Degas trademark is the unorthodox combination of traditional techniques, as in this 1877 pastel over monotype," a deep, masculine voice was explaining to the group.

Fran put down her sketch pad. The guy leading

the tour now gestured to the same painting she was copying. "Notice how the ephemeral medium of pastel gives an effect of movement and immediacy," he said.

Fran blinked.

Something about this tour *guide* was different.

She'd never seen him before, that was for certain—she would have remembered. Most of the Art Institute guides were middle-aged and scholarly-looking; he was young and more gorgeous than any guy Fran had ever seen in person. Longish golden hair was swept back from his high forehead. His eyes were a deep, mesmerizing blue, and he had chiseled, classically handsome features. And even though he wasn't speaking to her, his deep, rich voice seemed to wrap itself warmly around her, pulling her close.

"Degas also played tricks with perspective," the tour guide said. "See how we seem to be looking at the stage from the orchestra pit, alongside the musicians?"

Without thinking, Fran placed her pad and charcoal pencil on the bench and stood up. She was hypnotized.

"It's an intimate view too." The way he lingered on the word *intimate* caused a chill to run down Fran's spine. "Notice the dancers' loose hair," he went on. "We're catching them in the middle of a rehearsal."

Okay, forget what I said about not being interested in meeting random guys, Fran thought, her heart pounding. *I want to meet this guy.*

And he wasn't really random, she decided a few

seconds later as she slipped into the tour group so that she could hear and see him better. They were at the museum, not on the bus. He was a tour guide—an art expert! What could be more perfect?

The guy kept talking about Degas; Fran kept staring at him, trying unsuccessfully to read his name tag, which was twisted sideways and half hidden by his shirt pocket.

"So, think about that as we check out the next monotype," he suggested, smiling straight at Fran with perfect, bright white teeth.

For a brief moment their eyes locked, and Fran wondered if her feelings were written all over her face. *Can he tell I have an instant crush on him?* she wondered, her cheeks burning. *Can he tell he and I are made for each other?*

The tour guide concluded his remarks on Degas and herded the group to the next gallery. Fran was dying to follow them but, coming back down to earth a little, remembered that she'd left her sketching stuff just lying on the bench in the middle of the room. On top of that, she wasn't even part of the tour group, which at some point the guide might figure out. *And then how ridiculous would I look?* she thought.

The tour group disappeared, gorgeous guide and all.

My imagination must have invented him, Fran decided as she sat down and picked up her sketch pad and pencil again. *He's too good-looking to be true. And smart and totally inspirational when he talks about Degas.*

9

Not to mention older. Fran chewed thoughtfully on her pencil. He could be a college student, or maybe even in graduate school. Twenty? Twenty-two?

Too old for me either way, she thought with a sigh. Then again, maybe he wasn't. There was no law against daydreaming, was there? She could picture it perfectly: The guy had noticed her just now, and after the tour was over, he'd come back to find her. They'd go to lunch at the museum café and sit at one of those little tables, the kind where your knees always bumped into the other person's knees. They'd drink cappuccino and talk about art, and after a little while he'd take her hand and start caressing her fingers and then—

Fran blinked herself awake, blushing furiously. It was a pretty tame fantasy—Caley would die laughing—but *still* . . . In her whole life, Fran had never fallen for somebody so hard and so fast. And she hadn't even met him!

But I will meet him somehow, Fran promised herself. *And soon.* A smile touched her lips. Caley had scoffed at Fran's description of the perfect guy—she didn't believe he existed—but now Fran had definite proof that he did.

The tour guide, Fran thought, happily closing her eyes. *Now that's the kind of guy I could fall head over heels in love with. Easily.*

Two

FRAN AND THE hot tour guide were at the Louvre in Paris, standing in front of Leonardo da Vinci's *Mona Lisa*. His arms were wrapped tightly around her; her arms were lifted so she could rake her fingers through his thick golden hair. "Fran," he whispered in that deep, velvety voice. She tingled all over with anticipation. His perfect lips moved closer . . . closer . . .

Something woke Fran up. *Darn,* she thought, sleepily hugging her pillow. *I can't believe I missed it!*

Her eyes still closed, Fran listened to the summer morning sounds drifting in through her bedroom window. What had woken her up right at the crucial moment? The breeze rustling the leaves on the maple tree? A lawn mower buzzing in the distance? Birds singing?

Drea snoring.

Fran threw off her covers. So much for love at the Louvre.

11

She ate a quick breakfast, then put on a gauzy flowered skirt and tank top and locked herself in the bathroom—William and Douglas had a tendency to barge in without knocking. It was pretty early, but she was eager to get to the museum.

Ducking into her bedroom one last time to grab a sketch pad, Fran caught Drea rummaging in her dresser. "What are you doing?" she asked.

Drea whirled around, her expression guilty.

Fran's eyes widened when she saw what her stepsister was wearing. "Hey, that's my new shirt!"

Drea looked down at the cropped, rib-knit T-shirt. "Looks good with these jeans, don't you think?"

"That's not the point. I can't believe you took it without asking first!"

"Well, can I borrow it?" Drea asked.

"No!"

Sketch pad in hand, Fran stomped downstairs. Drea hung over the railing to call after her. "Since I can't wear the shirt, can I borrow your white sandals?"

"We don't even wear the same *size,* Drea."

"Close enough."

"Forget it," Fran declared, exasperated. "Just stay out of my stuff, okay?"

Fran's father appeared at the screen door a moment after it slammed shut behind her. "Hold on a minute," he said.

Fran waited while he stepped out onto the front porch. "What's up, Dad?"

Max Delaney ran a hand through his thick, graying hair. He was a tall, handsome man who managed to look distinguished even when he was wearing rumpled pajamas. "Fight with your sister?"

"I didn't start it," Fran said. "She doesn't respect my privacy at all, Dad."

"I know this is a big adjustment for you, Franny," he told her. "But maybe if you tried to be a little more flexible—"

His tone was mild, but Fran knew a lecture when she heard one. "I *am* trying," she interrupted. "But Drea is—" Fran stopped. She couldn't find the words to explain how much Drea bugged her.

"What?" her father asked.

"She's . . . eleven," Fran answered lamely. "We really, really don't have anything in common."

"Except you're part of the same family now."

Don't remind me, Fran thought. She knew it would make her dad happy if she said she loved having a step-sister. But she couldn't lie. "I know," she mumbled.

"All right, Franny." Her dad gave her a quick hug. "Off to the Art Institute?" he guessed.

She nodded, then stood on tiptoe to kiss his cheek. "See you on campus later."

As annoyed with Drea as she was, Fran instantly forgot all her irritation on the way to the bus stop. She was too busy plotting her morning.

Perfect, she thought, glancing at her watch. *I'll get to the museum before it opens, and maybe I'll see that gorgeous tour guide coming to work!*

As she expected, the Art Institute was still locked when she got there, so Fran sat down near one of the big stone lions that flanked the staircase

13

leading up to the entrance. Behind her, a row of colorful flags fluttered in the warm breeze; ahead of her, the whole skyline of Chicago was spread out, the skyscrapers glittering in the morning light.

It was great people-watching territory. Wrapping her arms around her knees, Fran scoped the traffic on the sidewalk. *Here comes a guy with blondish hair,* she thought, her nervous excitement growing. Her heart leaped, then sank with disappointment as he drew closer. *Nope, not the one.*

Is that him? she wondered a moment later. Squinting, she focused eagerly on a tall guy in khakis striding toward the museum. Again she heaved a disappointed sigh.

After a few minutes Fran heard the big door behind her clank open. She rose to go inside, casting one last glance over her shoulder.

That's when she saw him.

Him. The to-die-for tour guide.

Fran's heart did an excellent imitation of a kickboxing figure in one of her stepbrothers' Nintendo games.

Wow, she thought somewhat breathlessly as he jogged up the museum steps, her own feet frozen to the concrete. He was dressed more casually that day; he had on Tevas and gym shorts, so Fran got a good look at his suntanned, muscular legs.

The guy disappeared through the museum doors. Fran raced after him. She was on a mission. She had to find out where he was going. She had to find out who he *was.*

14

The guy headed down a hall to the Art Institute's administrative offices and then through a door marked Registration. Fran stopped outside. Peeking into the office, she could see him talking to a secretary.

"I want to register for the advanced life drawing class," she heard the guy say.

The secretary nodded. "You're just in time. The class is almost full—only two spaces left. Here," she said, handing him a form.

The guy scribbled quickly on the form, then turned to leave.

Fran panicked. *I can't let him catch me spying on him,* she thought. *How dumb would that look?* Ducking down the hall, she flattened herself against the wall a few yards back, hoping he'd walk in the other direction.

He did. *Do I follow him? Or grab the last spot in the drawing class?* Fran agonized. The class seemed like a golden opportunity to get to know her dream guy, but if she took the time to register for it, she'd lose sight of him.

Opting for delayed gratification, she stepped into the office. "Hi," she said to the secretary. "Is it too late to sign up for the advanced life drawing class?"

"As it happens, there's one space still available." The secretary studied Fran over the rims of her bifocals. "It is an advanced class. Do you have the prerequisites?"

"I've taken many classes at my high school," Fran answered, "and some at Northwestern too. I could send in a transcript if you want, or bring in my portfolio."

"No, it sounds like you're well prepared. Just fill out this form for me and you'll be all set."

Fran started filling in the form. "So, um, that guy who was just in here," she began awkwardly. It was killing her to know that the secretary had a piece of paper in her desk drawer with all sorts of facts about her dream guy, while Fran stood there too embarrassed to ask his name. "Uh, the tour guide?"

"Yes?"

"He's taking the class too?"

The secretary nodded. If she thought it was strange that Fran's cheeks were turning flamingo pink, she didn't let on. "The first class is Monday evening." She handed Fran another sheet of paper. "Here's a list of supplies the instructor would like you to bring. Any other questions?"

What's his name? Where does he live? Do I really have to wait until Monday night to see him again?

"Uh, no. Thanks," Fran said.

She headed back out into the hallway of the museum, jittery from the whole experience.

Okay. What should I do now? she wondered. The Art Institute was a big place. Should she start searching for him, gallery by gallery? *He might not even be leading tours today,* she realized, remembering his casual shorts and sandals. With a sigh, she glanced at a clock. Two hours until she needed to be at her research assistant job. She'd brought her sketching supplies . . . might as well sketch.

Fran wandered up to the European painting galleries and randomly settled down on a bench with a view of a fifteenth-century Spanish painting called *St. George Killing the Dragon*. It would be fun to sketch. Fran pulled out her book, looked up—and saw him.

The guy!

She'd been right about the shorts—he wasn't leading a tour that day. Instead, like her, apparently he was at the museum to draw.

He was sitting sideways, his eyes fixed on a Rubens painting of a voluptuous Madonna and child. Carefully staying out of his line of vision, Fran tiptoed close enough to sneak a look at his work. He was using pastels, and he was *good*. He'd sketched in the basic outlines of the composition, and the gestures and expressions of the central figures were perfect.

As Fran watched him in admiration, he drew the folds of Mary's gown with a few confident strokes of red pastel. Then he paused, his gaze lifted to the Rubens.

Now's a good time to introduce myself, Fran thought. *I could just say hi, and then maybe something like, "I think I signed up for the same drawing class as you." That wouldn't seem too weird. Or then again, I could have a shyness attack and be completely mute.*

Tongue-tied, Fran watched him for as long as she dared, drinking in his details with worshipful eyes: his gorgeous, perfect profile, the way his wavy hair swept the collar of his shirt in back, the sculpted, bronzed muscles of his biceps, his strong, sure fingers colored with pastel dust. Oh, and his artistic talent. That was pretty incredible too.

Wow, Fran thought dreamily. *Double wow.*

Three

"EVERYBODY READY TO go?" Fran's father asked after breakfast the next morning.

It was a sunny Saturday, with a steady breeze off the lake. Max had arranged to borrow a sailboat from a faculty friend, and Emma had packed a picnic. The twins and Drea had spent half an hour rummaging in the shed in the backyard, hunting up life preservers and other gear. Fran went through the motions, dressing in gym shorts, boat shoes, and an anorak. Now, though, as everybody else straggled out to the car for the short drive to the marina, she hung back.

"Coming, Fran?" Max asked.

Fran hesitated because she knew her dad would be disappointed. Then, getting up her nerve, she shook her head. "Actually, Dad . . . I think I'll skip it."

Max raised his eyebrows. "What do you mean?"

18

Fran stuck her hands in her shorts pockets and shrugged. "I guess I'm not in the mood to sail."

"But it's Pete Bittermeyer's boat," he said. "We haven't taken her out since last August. Remember how much fun we had that day?"

Of course Fran remembered. *We had fun because it was just the two of us,* she wanted to point out. But being trapped on a tiny yacht with Drea, Douglas, and William sounded like a complete nightmare. "I'll see you when you get back. And I'll clean the house while everybody's gone," she added as a peace offering.

Now Max frowned. "Fran, a lot of planning went into this. I really think you should—"

Emma, having dumped the picnic stuff in the car, walked back to the door in time to interrupt her husband. "Don't make a big deal out of it, Max," she said, pushing back a stray wisp of her curly dark hair. "Fran can make her own decisions."

"Well . . . ," Max grumbled.

Emma took Max's arm. "Come on. See you later, Fran," she called over her shoulder. "And please don't clean the house. Do something fun."

Fran felt a lump of irritation grow inside her as she watched Emma and Max get into the car. She hated how Emma had brushed everything off so quickly, telling both of them what to do. Not that Fran wanted to fight with her dad. But she resented Emma's butting in.

A minute later the engine of Max's old Pontiac rumbled to life. As the car backed out of the driveway,

Fran watched from the porch, her feelings a jumbled mix. On one hand, she was psyched to have gotten out of the sailing trip. But she also couldn't ignore the twinge of disappointment that began to gnaw at her. Under other circumstances, she'd have loved to spend the day out on the water in Professor Bittermeyer's boat.

The bottom line, Fran thought moodily, *is that I'm not sailing with Dad, but everybody else is.*

She spent the next few hours cleaning the house from top to bottom just because Emma had told her not to. Then, after lunch, in an attempt to cheer herself up, she rode her bike to the art supply store.

Once inside, she lingered in front of the pastels display, her thoughts floating to the tour guide and the prospect of finally meeting him during Monday night's drawing class. But not even that was enough to snap Fran out of her down mood.

Face it, Fran, she thought, *you'll never find the nerve to talk to him anyway.*

She did allow herself to break into a small smile, however, when she considered the possibility that he might be the one to strike up a conversation. Okay, so that was probably outside the bounds of reality, but still, a girl could dream, couldn't she?

Definitely, Fran told herself. *Especially when she's bummed out.*

Inspired by her dream guy's artwork, Fran bought an assortment of pastels at the store. Then, adding them to the collapsible easel and canvas stool strapped to the rack on the back of her bike, she pedaled east to the Evanston lakeshore.

The sky, which had started out so blue, was now boiling with clouds. The wind had picked up too, and it took Fran ten minutes to set up her easel at the right angle so that it wouldn't blow over.

Oh, well, Fran thought. *Nothing's going right today anyway.* She taped a piece of textured paper to the board on the easel, and then, sitting on the low folding stool a few feet from the bike path, she started experimenting with the pastels.

Right away Fran wished the tour guide were there, and not just for the obvious reasons. She was in desperate need of some pointers. Not knowing what to do, she made many different marks, using the end of a pastel stick and then its side. Next she tried rubbing the marks with a piece of paper towel. Then she layered one color over another. It started to look like mud.

Frustrated, Fran sighed heavily, ripping the paper from her easel and starting over with a new sheet. *How did he make it look so easy?* she wondered, biting her lip in concentration as she drew in the outlines of a landscape: water, sky, dunes, a couple of people on the beach, some seagulls.

She drew fast because the cloud patterns were changing minute by minute. The colors were difficult to capture, and she used every pastel in the box, layering and blending them to try to get just the right effect. At one point she stopped to stare at a sailboat zipping along the horizon. Was it her dad and Emma and the kids? Annoyance rising, Fran narrowed her eyes, then marked the boat on her drawing with a slash of black.

"Yuck," she said out loud.

"Actually," a voice behind her said, "I think it's pretty good."

Fran's entire body stiffened. The last thing she felt like doing was chatting with a stranger. Not that she ever enjoyed that type of thing, but that day she was especially not in the mood.

Still, when she turned to see who'd spoken, she smiled despite herself.

There was a guy about her own age on the bike path. A guy on a unicycle. A guy on a unicycle *juggling*.

As Fran watched with arched eyebrows, the guy threw in some show-offy flourishes. But when he tried to juggle behind his back, one of his tennis balls flew off at an angle. He reached for it, and the unicycle tilted crazily.

"Watch out!" Fran screamed.

She held her breath as all three balls sailed in different directions. The guy jumped off the unicycle, catching it with his toe just before it crashed to the pavement.

Fran exhaled in relief. Scooping up the tennis balls, the guy gave her a playful smile. "That never happens," he swore.

Fran smirked back at him. "I bet."

He rested the unicycle on the sand next to the bike path, tossing the balls alongside it. Then he walked over to Fran with one hand extended. "Toby Kalbhen," he said.

"Oh." Fran stood up to shake his hand, feeling kind of awkward, as she always did around guys. But when he smiled at her again, his gray-blue eyes twinkling, she felt more at ease.

Toby wasn't palpitation-inducing, like the guy from the museum, but he was kind of cute in an offbeat way. He was only an inch or two taller than Fran, and his short blond hair stood straight up. She also noticed that his nose was a little bit crooked.

"Fran Delaney," she said.

Toby waved at her easel. "Hope I didn't wreck your concentration."

Fran grimaced at the drawing, a new wave of frustration washing over her. "It doesn't matter. I wasn't getting anywhere."

"I wouldn't say that." Toby studied Fran's work. "Maybe you haven't used pastels before, but you know how to draw."

Fran raised her eyebrows. *What can a guy who juggles and rides a unicycle possibly know about art?*

"You're great with line and color," Toby went on. "You usually paint with acrylics or watercolors, right?"

Fran nodded, her mouth dropping slightly open. Who *was* this guy?

"Well, I should buzz out of here so you can get back to work," he said. But then he hesitated, giving her a look as if to ask, *Should I or shouldn't I?*

He wants to hang out and talk, Fran thought, and to her surprise, she realized she actually wanted him to.

"That's all right," Fran told him. She held up a pastel stick. "I was just messing around trying to figure out how to use these things. I'm ready to quit."

"No way. You should finish this. It's cool—it expresses a lot of emotion, you know?" Toby looked from the easel to Fran, his eyes speculative. "Anger, maybe? Loneliness?"

Fran stared at her picture. Was there something lurking there, in the wild clouds and dark slash of a sailboat?

Then she felt her cheeks flame up. The drawing was supposed to be an innocent landscape—it wasn't supposed to say anything about herself. With a quick motion, she ripped the paper off her easel. "It stinks," she murmured.

"I didn't mean to embarrass you," he said.

"I'm not embarrassed," Fran protested, but she cast her eyes down and pretended to be busy putting away the pastels. "How come you know so much about art anyway?"

"My brother's into it, and I draw a comic strip for my school newspaper," Toby explained.

"Really?" Fran pushed her blond hair away from her face, looking back at Toby with increased interest. *Have I seen this guy around?* she wondered. "Do you go to Lakeview North?" she asked.

"South," he answered. "I'll be a junior."

"Me too," Fran said. "I mean, at North." She smiled at the fact that they were the same exact age. But then she suddenly felt silly, and her smile disappeared. *Why do you care?* she wondered. *You don't even know him. And you might not want to. I mean, what's with the unicycle?*

Her expression must have changed while she was having these thoughts, because Toby then broke into a grin. "You're wondering what's with the unicycle, right?"

For the second time that day Fran's mouth dropped open. "No! I mean, I was just . . ." Fran drifted off, at a loss. Then she shook her head. "Okay, you caught me," she admitted. "Do you have a summer job with the circus or something?"

"I'm a camp counselor at the Y, if that counts," Toby replied. He reached down to pluck a stalk of dune grass, then started chewing on it. "I saw this guy riding one once and I thought, hey, I bet I could do that. So I asked him if I could try it."

"And you liked it?"

"Sure. It's a funky way to get places, you know? Gives me a different view of the world."

Fran tipped her head to one side, smiling skeptically. Toby managed to make this all sound almost reasonable. "Okay," Fran said. "The juggling part, though. That's definitely nuts."

"You should've seen me a week ago," Toby said with a laugh. "I couldn't do it at all. Now I'm getting pretty good, if I do say so myself."

"You just taught yourself how?"

"Yep."

"Why?"

He shrugged, taking the stalk of grass from his mouth and tossing it. "If I'm not learning new stuff all the time, even something brainless like juggling, I go crazy." He eyed her, that playful smile on his face again. "Don't you ever feel like that?"

Fran thought about this. The pastels had been something new, but her main reason for that experiment had been the gorgeous tour guide. Her step-family was new, and she could definitely live without them. "No," she said. "I guess I don't."

While they'd been talking, the sky had grown darker. Now Fran felt raindrops on her bare arms. "That decides it—I *am* done sketching," she said.

"And I'm done juggling."

While Toby stowed his tennis balls in his backpack, Fran folded up her easel and strapped it onto the bike rack. Then she turned back to him. "Well . . . ," she said, surprised that she was actually slightly bummed to say good-bye to him. He had been fun to talk to.

"Well . . . ," Toby echoed.

Fran climbed onto her bike, balancing with one foot on the pavement. "See you around," she said, putting her foot to the pedal.

"Uh . . . Fran?"

Fran dropped her foot back to the ground. "Yeah?"

Toby ran a hand through his damp hair. It was raining harder now. "What do you say we make sure of it?" he asked with a hopeful-looking smile. "I mean, seeing each other around. Would you give me your phone number?"

Fran burst into a grin, feeling an unexpected surge of pleasure. "Okay." She wrote her name with a pastel stick on a scrap of paper. "Here."

Toby folded the note carefully and stuck it in his shirt pocket. "I'll call you," he told her. "Maybe we could do something next weekend." There was that teasing smile again. "I can tell you're dying for unicycle lessons."

"Right." Fran laughed. "Well, so long."

"So long."

They pedaled off in opposite directions. Fran rode fast, blinking the raindrops out of her eyes. She'd gotten over being disappointed about not sailing with her father and about bombing out with pastels. She didn't even mind that she was soaking wet. She was too busy smiling as she thought back over her conversation with Toby.

So it wasn't the kind of flirtatious interlude Caley was always having with random guys. But maybe this was better. After all, Fran already had her sights set on the tour guide in terms of romance. Whether that was realistic or not, she knew she wasn't going to let go of that fantasy for a very long time. If ever.

No, Toby wasn't her type. But he did make her smile, and she did look forward to seeing him again. She'd never had a close guy friend before—maybe that was what Toby would become.

He had been so easy to talk to, so funny. Not like any guy she'd ever met. Her whole interaction with him had been so out of the ordinary.

And I'm going to see him again next weekend, Fran thought as she turned onto her street, the feeling of quiet excitement making her warm despite the rain.

Four

"GUESS WHAT I'M doing tomorrow?" Fran asked Caley on Sunday night. Her best friend had been away all weekend, visiting her aunt and uncle, but they'd met up that night to go to the movies.

"What?" Caley asked.

"Taking a life drawing class—with the guy of my dreams." Fran waited for her friend's shocked reaction. She hadn't even told Caley about her crush on the guy from the museum yet, although she knew all about the new guy Caley liked.

Caley fixed her with a serious gaze and said, "Spill. And I want details."

As they waited in line to buy tickets, Fran described her two near-encounters with the gorgeous tour guide—whom Caley quickly dubbed "Museum Guy"—and her impulsive registration for the drawing class.

"I mean, it's destiny. He's the perfect guy I was describing just the other day!" Fran gushed. "Gorgeous *and* an artist!"

"A tour guide, huh? Doesn't that make him old?" Caley asked.

"Not necessarily *old*. Older, but maybe only by a couple of years. I don't know why, but I just have this feeling that it doesn't matter."

"Sounds like you have *lots* of feelings about this guy," Caley said with a suggestive wiggle of her eyebrows.

Fran giggled. "It's totally not like me, right? You should see him, though." They moved inside to the concession line. "He draws really, really well, and he was so intense when he talked about Degas." Fran lowered her voice. "And he has these blue eyes. And this *body*."

"Better grab some extra napkins," Caley teased. "You're drooling."

"Caley!" Fran exclaimed, but she laughed anyway. Their turn came at the counter. "So what am I going to do?" she asked.

"Order a soda," Caley suggested, "and we can split a popcorn."

Fran rolled her eyes. "I mean about Museum Guy."

"You jump on him," Caley advised as they collected their snacks and headed for the theater. "Or at least talk to him. I can't believe you didn't go for it when you saw him drawing."

"I couldn't," Fran admitted. "I was paralyzed. I was afraid I'd just babble like an idiot."

"Well, you made one good move. That drawing class will be your big chance."

Fran had thought so too, but as they hunted in the theater for good seats, she was suddenly overwhelmed by self-doubt. "What if he does turn out to be, like, ten years older than me or something?" She remembered the guy Caley had admired on the bus. Her heart sank. "Or married?"

"You won't know until you ask."

Fran shook her head. "I'll never be able to get up the nerve."

"You're planning to spend the whole summer panting over him from a distance?"

Fran wrinkled her nose. She felt like a loser, but she had to tell the truth. "It's possible."

"Fran!" Caley laughed. "You have to be more motivated. Follow my lead. By the end of the day on Monday I promise I'll know Messenger Guy's name *and* phone number." Caley liked the bicycle delivery guy at her office.

"Well, maybe Messenger Guy is just more . . . approachable," Fran said as they settled into their seats.

They started munching popcorn. "Museum Guy is human too," Caley reasoned. "So he's artsy and a total stud, which for you is a killer combination, but that doesn't mean he's a god."

But he is a god, Fran thought. *He's everything I've ever wanted in a guy.* She knew she couldn't explain to Caley, who was never shy around guys, how impossible it was to picture herself chatting flirtatiously with Museum Guy the way Caley

30

would chat and flirt with Messenger Guy.

"Hey—how was your weekend anyway?" Caley asked. "What did you do? Aside from miss me, of course."

"Actually . . ." Fran smiled to herself. Caley was going to like this story. "I met a guy."

"No way!" Caley exclaimed. "*Another* guy? When? Who? Tell me everything!"

Fran giggled at her friend's excitement. "Well, I was at the beach Saturday afternoon, sketching. And this guy came up to me on a unicycle. Oh—and he was juggling. We just talked for a while. He goes to South. His name's Toby."

"And?" Caley pressed.

"And . . . nothing. He was nice."

"Good-looking?"

"Not bad. Above average. But mainly he was just a cool guy—I could really see us being friends. I didn't feel shy around him, like I usually am around guys," Fran explained. "At the end, it started to rain and we both got soaked. That's when I gave him my phone number."

"That's my girl!" Caley teased.

Fran giggled again. "I knew you'd be proud."

"So you gave him your number, but you think you just want to be friends?" Caley asked.

Fran bit her lip. "Yes."

"Saving yourself for Museum Guy, huh?"

"Well . . . yeah," Fran admitted.

"But you still haven't even *spoken* to him," Caley reminded her.

31

"So? If—or when—we finally get together, it'll be awesome."

"Well, I wouldn't write Toby off if I were you," Caley advised. "There's nothing wrong with juggling two guys at once."

"Caley!" Fran shook her head at the ridiculousness of it. Her, Fran Delaney, juggling *two* guys? That was highly unlikely. Besides, she'd be happy with just one. The perfect one.

Fran had planned to get to the Art Institute about ten minutes before class on Monday. She wanted to have time to check her makeup in the bathroom and then snag an easel next to Museum Guy's, maybe even try to talk to him before class started. But traffic was so horrible that instead of being early, she was five minutes late. By the time she rushed breathlessly into the studio where the class was being held, every easel but one was taken.

The one farthest from Museum Guy.

The other students had already taped paper to their boards and had started sketching the model.

The instructor approached Fran, glancing at the list on her clipboard. "I'm Brigitte," she said. "And you are . . . Fran?"

Fran nodded. "Sorry I'm late."

Brigitte was middle-aged but extremely cool-looking, with cropped gray hair and very red lipstick. "That's okay. We already went around the room and made introductions, but I'm sure you'll meet everyone as we go along. Tonight we're starting with quick, three-minute poses. Ready to jump right in?"

Fran darted a glance at Museum Guy, who was drawing rapidly, his eyes glued to the model. *I can't believe I missed introductions,* she thought miserably.

"Yes," she told the teacher.

They drew for forty-five minutes, then Brigitte gave a brief lecture while the model went on a break. After that the whole class took a break. Some people headed to the rest rooms or the café, while others sat around chatting. Museum Guy got into an animated conversation with two women whose easels were near his. Fran couldn't help noticing that one of them was young and very pretty, with big dark eyes and waist-length black hair. Museum Guy was bound to notice too—any guy would.

I can't let her steal my chance with him, Fran thought, wishing Caley were there to give her a pep talk and a kick in the rear. She simply had to wander over there and casually listen in. How hard could it be?

It turned out to be impossible. Fran fiddled with her box of charcoal sticks for a minute, mentally rehearsing her opening line: *Haven't I seen you around the museum?* Bad. *This is my first drawing class here. How about you?* Worse. *I have a car tonight. Want to go for a drive and make out?*

Shaking her head at her inability to think of anything normal to say, she went out into the hall for a drink at the water fountain. When she came back in, the model was ready to pose again.

It was good experience to draw a live model, but

Fran didn't exactly make the most of the evening artistically. Her gaze kept sneaking across the room to Museum Guy, and, more often than not, his body was the one that would materialize on her paper instead of the model's.

As the end of class drew near, Fran devised a strategy. The night wouldn't be a total waste if she could arrange to bump into Museum Guy at the door, make some significant eye contact, or at least overhear somebody calling him by name.

No such luck. Fran was careful to throw her supplies together as fast as she could, but Museum Guy was faster. He was the first one out the door, and the pretty black-haired girl was right behind him. By the time Fran hurried into the hall, both Museum Guy and the girl had disappeared.

She drove home in a state of complete despair. "I blew it," she said miserably, pounding her fist on the steering wheel. "Three whole hours and I still don't even know his name!" Meanwhile, had Museum Guy gone out for a cup of coffee or something with the pretty dark-eyed girl after class?

At home, the light was off in Fran and Drea's room. Fran tiptoed around as she undressed in the moonlight. Before climbing into bed, she slipped a piece of crumpled-up paper out from her art portfolio and smoothed out the wrinkles. It was one of the quick charcoal sketches she'd made of Museum Guy during class that night.

Fran taped the picture up over one of Drea's James Van Der Beek posters. Lying in bed, she stared up at the faint, impressionistic figure of Museum Guy floating over her, her heart aching. Had she lost him to someone else before their romance had even begun?

"It's a six-week class, right?" Caley said the next night after dinner. "Next time, just make sure to grab an easel near his."

The two girls sat on the rug in Fran's bedroom, their backs propped against her bed as they listened to CDs.

"But there's this really pretty girl." Fran slumped down, her legs stretched out in front of her, and stared glumly at her pink-painted toenails. "She's hitting on him already."

Caley dismissed this concern with a wave. "She can't be half as pretty as you, Franny." She stood up to switch tracks on the CD. "What about Toby? Has he called yet?"

Suddenly the bedroom door swung open and banged loudly against the wall. "Has who called yet?" Drea demanded.

Fran rolled her eyes as Drea draped herself across the other bed. "Nobody," Fran said.

"Come on," Drea pleaded. "You can tell me."

Fran folded her arms across her chest. Trust Drea not to take a hint. "You know, we were having a private discussion," Fran said.

"This is my room too," Drea countered.

Fran sighed. She knew from experience that this was a losing battle. If she tried to kick Drea out, her stepsister would go running to Emma, and Fran would get in trouble. "What were we talking about?" Fran asked, turning back to Caley.

"You know who."

"Oh. Right. No, he hasn't called." Even though Fran spent most of her time thinking about Museum Guy, she was a little disappointed that she hadn't heard from Toby yet.

"Why don't you call him?" Caley asked.

Fran shrugged. "He didn't give me his number."

"Who?" Drea asked.

"Look him up in the book," Caley said, ignoring Drea.

"I couldn't." It had been surprisingly easy to talk to Toby that day at the beach, but calling him up cold would be an entirely different matter. "I wouldn't know what to say."

Drea bounced a little on her bed. "To who?" she exclaimed. "Who *is* he?"

Fran gritted her teeth, resisting the urge to smother Drea with a pillow. "Wanna take a walk?" she asked Caley, jumping to her feet. It seemed to be the only way to get away from her annoying stepsister.

"Yeah, let's get ice cream," Caley replied.

"I could go for ice cream," Drea said, her eyes lighting up.

"We'll bring some back for you," Fran told her.

Before Drea could protest, Fran and Caley ran out of Fran's room, ducking out of the house as quickly as possible.

"I know this is mean," Fran panted as they ran down the block laughing, "but I had to get away from her!"

Out of sight of Fran's house, they slowed to a walk. It was a warm evening—the last rays of sunset filtered hazily through the leaves of the trees lining Elm Street. "What are you going to do about her?" Caley asked.

Fran shrugged. "What can I do? I'm stuck with her."

"You could talk to Emma and your dad," Caley suggested. "When I used to share a room with Colleen, before Mara went to college, my parents made up this rule. We each got the room to ourselves for an hour every day. When it was my hour, Colleen had to do stuff someplace else."

It sounded like a decent idea. An hour a day was better than nothing. "Maybe I will talk to them," Fran said. "Someday."

When the phone rang Thursday night, Fran sauntered over to pick it up. It was a relief not to have to race with Drea to answer the phone—she was over at a friend's house.

"Hello?" she said.

"Is this Fran?" a guy's voice asked. "It's Toby Kalbhen. From the beach last weekend."

To her surprise, Fran's heart did a tiny cartwheel. Holding the cordless to one ear, she sank into an easy chair in the family room, her legs hooked over the chair's arm. *I'm just excited because I don't get phone calls from guys very often,* she thought, trying to make herself relax. "Hi. How're you doing?"

"Pretty good." Toby made a funny sound, half cough, half throat clearing. *Is he nervous?* Fran wondered. "So, uh, last weekend . . ." There was that sound again. "We, um, talked about maybe getting together? Do you still want to? Or maybe you don't even remember?"

He is *nervous,* Fran thought, and for some reason that struck her as extremely sweet. "Of course I remember," she said with a laugh. "What did you have in mind?"

"I just thought lunch? On Saturday, around noon? Pizza at Giordano's? Sound okay?"

"Sounds fine," Fran assured him.

"Great," Toby said again. "Well . . . cool!"

She laughed again, now completely relaxed. "So, how was camp today?" she asked.

"You have a good memory," Toby said. "It was okay. I'm the drama counselor, and today we did these skits where the kids all pretended to be famous people in Chicago, like the mayor and Michael Jordan and stuff—it was very funny."

"Sounds like it."

"Do you have a summer job?" Toby asked.

"I'm a research assistant for an art history professor at Northwestern," Fran told him. "This guy who works with my dad."

"Wow," Toby said. "Sounds like a total brain-a-thon."

"Does it?" Fran asked, wondering if she was

coming across as nerdy and serious. "Maybe it is a little. I just wanted to do something over vacation that tied in with my interests."

"That's cool," Toby said. "I didn't mean to sound like everybody should be a camp counselor. You can tell me more about it on Saturday, okay?"

"Okay," Fran said.

"Well . . . thanks for talking to me, Fran."

She laughed. "No problem."

"See you in two days."

"Right," she agreed. Her heart did one more little cartwheel. "Two days."

After they'd hung up, Fran sat for a few minutes hugging a throw pillow, a smile lingering on her face. Toby wasn't anything like Museum Guy, but still, she was psyched at the prospect of seeing him again.

Two days, she thought. *I kind of wish it were just one.*

Five

I'M GLAD DREA'S not around to spy on me while I get ready for this date, Fran thought on Saturday as noon crept closer. Emma had driven Drea and the twins up to Winnetka to spend the day with their dad. *Not that this is a date, really.*

Fran pulled a black-and-white flowered skirt from her closet, then pushed it back into the rack. *I mean, we're just going to Giordano's.* She considered a pair of dressy shorts with a matching vest, then finally settled on a short denim jumper. *This is just, like, casual. Like going out to lunch with Caley or something.*

She still felt anxious when she walked into Giordano's, though. And as she nervously scanned faces in search of Toby's, she had a moment of panic. *I've only actually spoken to him in person once,* she thought. *What if this is totally awkward?*

Then she spotted him—he'd already snagged a booth—and her worry melted away.

"Hey," he said, giving her the warm, engaging smile she remembered from the beach. His blue-gray eyes crinkled. "Good to see you."

He stood up, putting out a hand. Fran shook it, her elbow jerking stiffly. "This feels a little formal," she joked.

Toby snatched his hand back, grinning. "You're right. Forget I did that. Just sit down and we'll argue about pepperoni versus sausage as if we've known each other forever."

Fran slid into the booth across from Toby. "Obviously we haven't known each other forever or you'd know I don't eat pepperoni *or* sausage."

"No kidding. You're a vegetarian?"

"Just when it comes to pizza," she explained. "I always get the same thing: green peppers, black olives, and extra cheese."

He cocked one eyebrow. "*Always?*"

"Always."

"Then that's what we'll order." Toby slapped his menu shut. "Large."

"Large? You don't think that's too much for two people?"

"Not when one of the people has been juggling all morning," he said. "I'm starved."

After they ordered, Toby folded his arms on top of the table and leaned forward. "So, how was your week? Anything exciting happen?"

"Well . . . I did start taking this cool drawing class at the Art Institute." Toby looked interested, and Fran immediately felt stupid for bringing it up.

It wasn't as though she could talk to Toby about Museum Guy or anything. Her cheeks flushed, and she quickly changed the subject. "Anyway, I want to know more about this cartoon thing. Like, how do you do it?"

Toby pulled a paper napkin from the dispenser. "Got a pen?"

She took a pen from her bag and handed it to him. Toby scribbled something on the napkin. It only took a minute, and then he pushed the napkin across the table toward her.

Fran turned it around, smiling when she saw the drawing. There were two stylized cartoon figures—a guy and a girl—sitting in a booth at a restaurant. They had bugged-out eyes and wild hair. "I love the sideways noses," she said, laughing.

"All my cartoon characters have broken noses, like me," Toby explained. "It's kind of my trademark."

"How'd you break yours?" she asked, studying his face. She thought that Toby's crooked nose wasn't a negative thing at all—it gave his face an imperfect, offbeat charm.

"When I was four and he was about seven, my big brother pushed me down the stairs." Toby smiled. "*Accidentally*, of course."

"Of course." Fran laughed. "Draw some more," she urged.

Toby obliged. This time, the guy cartoon character was on a unicycle; the girl was at an easel. "You're really good," Fran said, impressed. "Did you learn how to do this in a class?"

"Nah." Toby stuck the cap back on the pen. "I'm not into that kind of thing."

"Why not?"

"It's not my style," he explained. "I like to learn stuff just by doing it."

Fran thought about that. That was what she'd tried to do the other day at the beach with the pastels, and she had failed miserably. "I think I do better when I take a class and somebody teaches me," she confessed. "I don't know why."

Their pizza came, and they each took a slice. "Nothing wrong with a class if your teacher's got some imagination," Toby said. "Your dad's an art history professor, right?"

Fran nodded.

"How about your mom—what does she do?" Toby asked.

Fran looked down at her plate. At some point she always had to share this with new friends, but it never got any easier. "My mom's dead," she said quietly.

"Oh. I'm sorry," Toby said, his voice softer too.

Fran looked back up at him. His eyes were warm and filled with concern. "It's okay. She died a long time ago. To tell you the truth, I don't even remember her that well."

"That must make you sad."

Fran didn't usually talk about this, but somehow she didn't mind discussing it with Toby. "Yeah. It does." Then she added, "But I have a stepmother now, for what that's worth."

"Ah," Toby said, nodding. "I see." He seemed

to sense that this was a sore topic for Fran and changed the subject. They chatted for a while about other stuff: schools, friends, hobbies.

Fran had to laugh as Toby listed the activities he was involved with. "Let's see—marching band, karate, drama club, Spanish club, helping at the soup kitchen," she repeated. "Oh, and juggling and riding your unicycle. What's the pattern here?"

Toby flashed his off-center grin. "There should be a pattern?"

Fran shook her head, smiling. "Okay, maybe not, but do you have time to sleep?"

"Enough," Toby said. "But that's not even everything. I've got this other great idea."

"Well, what is it?"

"Okay. I've been thinking about how I live in this incredibly diverse place," Toby began. "But all my friends are kind of like me. You know, relatively privileged. Ballet lessons, cello lessons, school plays, drawing classes at the Art Institute, that kind of thing. See what I'm getting at?"

Fran shook her head. "Not really."

Toby rested his elbows on the table and leaned forward, his eyes growing intense and serious. "My point is, there have to be tons of other kids—inner-city kids—who could be saxophonists or sculptors or tap dancers, but they just don't get exposed to that kind of stuff. But what if I started an outreach program? I could match kids like us—artists, dancers, musicians—with kids like them."

"Wow," Fran said. She'd been expecting him to

say that he was going to learn how to play the harmonica or something. This was a lot heavier. Not to mention a whole lot more ambitious.

Toby wrinkled his nose. "Sounds totally out there, doesn't it?"

It did, a little. But that wasn't what surprised Fran most. She'd pegged Toby as a carefree type. "It's a pretty big switch from unicycles and juggling. You really want to do something that serious?"

"Sure." Toby took a sip of his Sprite. "Why, does it sound like I think I'm some kind of superhero trying to save the world?"

Fran smiled. "A little. But so what? It's cool. I mean, I don't know anybody else our age who would even think of doing something like that. You know, try to change people's lives." Fran included herself in that comment. She could never do anything like the project Toby had envisioned.

Toby shrugged. "It's still really half-baked. You're the first person I've told about it, actually."

Fran felt flattered. She ran her finger around the rim of her glass. "Well, let me know how it turns out."

He nodded, his eyes brightening. "I will."

They finished their pizza and split the bill, then walked outside. "I wish I had time for a walk or a movie or something," Toby told Fran as they stood on the sidewalk in front of Giordano's, "but I have to go tutor this kid, Jerome, from camp."

"Oh." Fran felt an unexpected rush of disappointment at his words. "Well, maybe we could see each other again sometime," she blurted out. "Like, next weekend or something."

Fran blushed at her own forwardness, but Toby responded with an enthusiastic smile. "Cool," he said. "Next weekend. Definitely!" He shook her hand good-bye, which made them both laugh.

Walking home by herself, Fran still couldn't believe she'd put the moves on Toby that way. She also couldn't believe that for the entire hour and a half while she'd been having lunch with him, she hadn't thought once about Museum Guy.

That doesn't mean I'm not still crazy about Museum Guy, because I am, she thought as she strolled up to her front door. *But it means* something.

The next morning Fran and Caley went out for waffles. "All right, you've kept me waiting long enough," Caley declared as she reached for the syrup pitcher. "Tell me all about Toby."

Fran smiled. "I like him," she confessed. "I mean, I knew I liked him or else I wouldn't have wanted to hang out with him, but I wasn't sure I was going to *like* him. And I liked him more than I thought I would."

Caley grinned with her mouth full of waffle. When she was finished chewing, she said, "So? What's he like?"

"He drew me this cartoon on a paper napkin," Fran said. "And he told me all this stuff he dreams about doing, like teaching art to poor kids in the projects. He was just really thoughtful and funny." Her face softened, remembering. "Like when I mentioned that my mom died. Some people, when they find that out, get really uncomfortable. They wish they hadn't asked. But I could tell Toby wanted to hear about it."

"He sounds adorable," Caley said, cutting a strip of bacon in half with her fork. "Maybe this is the guy, Franny."

Fran speared a strawberry with her fork and dunked it in the whipped cream on top of her waffles. She liked Toby. Definitely. *But I didn't fall in love at first sight,* she thought. *If it was anything remotely close to love, I wouldn't still be thinking about someone else, right?* "Toby can't be the guy because Museum Guy's the guy," she reminded her friend.

"Oh, right. Museum Guy," Caley said. "But you haven't even *met* him yet."

"It's just a matter of time," Fran responded. She took a big bite of her waffle. "Anyway, what's up with Messenger Guy?"

Caley's lips pursed in a frustrated pout. "His name's Miles something or other. He's always flying in and out of the office, too busy to talk." She sipped her iced coffee. "We were talking about you, though. Want my advice?"

"You'll give it to me whether I want it or not, won't you?" Fran asked.

Caley grinned. "Right. So this is it. Forget Museum Guy. Go for it with the real guy instead of pining after the fantasy one."

"But it's fun to fantasize about Museum Guy!" Fran protested.

47

Caley chuckled. "You're hopeless!"

An hour later Fran was still thinking over Caley's advice. Her room was quiet for once—Emma had taken Drea clothes shopping—so she flopped down on her bed, her arms folded behind her head, and stared at the leafy patterns of light and shadow on her ceiling. *Go for it with the real guy,* Caley had said.

But Museum Guy is real too, Fran thought. *Just in a different way.*

Fran felt her eyelids droop a little. The big brunch had made her drowsy. *I wonder what Toby's doing right now,* she thought sleepily. She pictured him on his unicycle, juggling. Or maybe he was drawing cartoons. Then another guy's image took over, completely monopolizing her imagination. Museum Guy at an easel in drawing class . . . leading a tour at the museum . . .

Fran closed her eyes. *What if I finally talk to him in class tomorrow night? We'll make a date to get together and draw. We'll talk about art and he'll fall madly in love with me and ask me to model for him. He'll paint a masterpiece, inspired by our endless, eternal love.*

As she pictured his portrait of her hanging on the walls of the Art Institute, Fran laughed out loud. She knew that was ridiculous—it was *all* ridiculous. Caley had told her to stop fantasizing about Museum Guy, and it was probably good advice. Still . . .

Can I forget about Museum Guy, Fran wondered, *even if I wanted to?*

Six

JUST DIAL, FRAN told herself midway through the next week. She'd double-checked that none of her stepsiblings was around, and now she sat at the kitchen table, the phone in her hand.

She was about to call Toby for the first time. He'd called her twice since their pizza date, but it was a totally different thing being the initiator. Fran's palms were sweaty.

She punched in the first three digits of Toby's number, then hit the off button. *Why am I doing this, anyhow?* she wondered. Was it just because so far she'd had a rotten week Museum Guy–wise? He hadn't been in drawing class Monday night, which had been a major bummer. Twice Fran had spotted him leading a tour, but she hadn't been able to get close enough to read his name tag.

That's part of it, Fran acknowledged. *But not all of it. If it were, I wouldn't be so worked up.*

She dialed the first three digits again, hesitated, then punched in the rest. The phone rang a few times, then somebody picked up. A guy's deep voice said, "Hello?"

It didn't sound like Toby. "Um . . . can I speak to Toby?" she asked.

"Sure. Hold on."

While she waited, her heart hammering, for Toby to come to the phone, Fran wondered if that had been his father or his brother. *His brother,* she decided. The guy had sounded mature, but not *that* mature.

"Hello?" Toby said, jolting Fran back to reality.

"Toby? It's Fran."

"Fran! What's up?"

Fran's spine collapsed with relief. She couldn't feel nervous when Toby sounded so glad, as though she'd just made his day by calling. "Just thought I'd say hi," she said. "Anything new with you?"

"A scrape on my nose," he answered. "I fell off the unicycle right onto my face."

Fran winced. "Maybe it's time to switch back to two wheels, huh?"

"No way," he declared. "Toby Kalbhen never quits."

"Even when you may end up needing plastic surgery?" Fran kidded.

He laughed. "Yes. Even then. So what'd you do today?"

Fran yawned just thinking about it. "Sorted through all these slides Professor Baird uses for his lectures and filed a bunch of old journal articles. It was pretty boring."

"Is it usually more fun?"

"No," she admitted. Fran was definitely disappointed in her summer job. "It's always pretty dry stuff. I thought it would be cool working for Professor Baird because he's so famous. You know, like his genius might rub off on me or something," she joked. "But talking to him is like talking to a textbook."

"Well, are you learning stuff?" Toby asked.

"Some," she said. "But I'm happier at the Art Institute. I go there almost every day."

"What's the big draw?" Toby asked. "I mean, there are lots of other museums in the city."

Fran flushed guiltily just thinking about the "big draw." "It's the paintings," she said quickly, fighting away the image of Museum Guy that had just popped into her head. "The Art Institute has the best collection."

"And you just look at them?"

"I sketch," she explained. "I do studies of the ones I like the best. It's like working for Professor Baird—it's one of the ways I'm teaching myself to be an artist."

"Hmmm," Toby said. "Know what I think?"

"What?"

"After being cooped up inside so much, you need to spend Saturday outdoors. With me."

Fran laughed. "Oh, yeah?"

"Yeah. What do you think about the Lincoln Park Zoo?"

Fran laughed again. "You want to go there?"

"Sure. Don't you like animals?"

For some reason, she continued to laugh. "Of course I do. Okay, let's go to the zoo."

As soon as she hung up with Toby, Fran called Caley. "Guess who I just talked to?" she asked.

"Isn't that, like, the third time this week?" Caley asked. "You guys are a couple already!"

"We're *not* a couple," Fran protested. Still, her face grew warm. "But we are going to the zoo on Saturday."

"That's so sweet!" Caley exclaimed. "Hey, you know what? I think I'll just have to happen to be at your house when he comes to pick you up."

Fran giggled. "Don't you think that will be a little obvious? What will we tell him?"

"That I came over to borrow something to wear," Caley told her. "Which might even be true, because I plan on asking Miles out for Saturday."

Fran laughed again, but she said okay. After all, she really did want Caley to meet Toby.

After she hung up the phone, she stood looking out her bedroom window at a distant sliver of blue lake. *Toby and I are going out on Saturday,* she mused. *And Caley's going to meet him.* It did seem as if they were on their way to being a real couple, which made Fran shiver with excitement.

But where does that leave Museum Guy? My first and deepest crush this summer?

On Saturday morning Fran and Caley waited on Fran's porch for Toby to pick her up. The two friends had everything perfectly planned—Caley had just enough time to meet Toby briefly before dashing off for her own date with Miles.

"Stop chewing your nails," Caley ordered.

Fran looked down at her fingers. That was her one bad nervous habit. "Was I? I didn't even notice." She pushed her blond hair behind her ears and smoothed the skirt of her short rayon dress. "How do I look?"

Caley smiled. "Beautiful. Like always."

Just then an old white Chevy van pulled up at the curb. "It's him," Fran whispered, spotting Toby behind the wheel.

Toby jumped out and walked over to them. "Hey, Fran," he said with an easy smile.

"Hi, Toby," Fran responded as he climbed the porch steps. "This is my friend Caley."

Caley gave him a little hello wave, but Toby didn't let her get away with that—he did the whole handshake thing, which made Caley laugh.

"Caley came over to borrow a shirt, and she decided to stick around to meet you," Fran explained.

Toby nodded, his gray-blue eyes looking especially blue that day. "And to check me out," he stated.

"No!" both girls protested at the same time, but Toby just shook his head and laughed.

"It's okay," he said, "I understand. Besides, I want to meet your friends, Fran."

Fran smiled. For some reason this made her very happy.

Toby looked at Caley. "So? Do I pass?"

"Hmmm," Caley teased, grinning. "I guess so."

"Phew." Toby wiped his forehead in a gesture of mock relief.

"You guys are headed for the zoo?" Caley asked.

"Actually, I found out there's this multicultural festival in the park next to the zoo," Toby said. "That might be more interesting." He looked back at Fran. "That is, if you're up for it."

Fran shrugged. She was usually a stickler for routine, but she liked how Toby made everything up as he went along. It was . . . *fun.* "Sure," she said. "Why not?"

"Cool." Toby broke into another smile.

They said their good-byes to Caley and started on their way. But Caley didn't let Fran get into Toby's car before mouthing the words "He's great!" to her.

Fran grinned to herself, watching Toby as he started up the car. *He is great, isn't he?* she thought.

But then she thought of Museum Guy—she couldn't help it—and how he fit every requirement she had in a guy.

I guess the question, Fran thought as she adjusted her seat belt, *is not whether Toby's great. It's whether he's right for me.*

By the time they got to the festival, Fran had stopped worrying whether Toby was her perfect match or not. After a couple of minutes of feeling tense in the car, she had resolved to just relax and have a good time.

Which was exactly what she was doing at the moment. Fran's eyes lit up as she looked around, taking in the sights of the festival. There were tons of different food booths lined up, forming a semicircle in the park. A large outdoor stage sat in the gap between the booths, and colorful flags representing all different countries flew against the clear blue sky. As hordes of people milled about— laughing, dancing, and eating—Fran took it all in, amazed that she had never come here before.

Toby nudged her. "You hungry?" he asked.

Fran nodded. "Sure. I could eat," she said, scanning the vendors for one that served American fare.

Toby pointed. "They've got Cajun over there. Or Thai—I could go for that."

"Do you see any hot dogs?" she asked hopefully.

"Hot dogs?" Toby raised an eyebrow. "We're at an *ethnic* food festival, Ms. Delaney. Let's get a little more adventurous! What'll it be, jambalaya or pad thai?"

"I've never tried either," Fran admitted, crossing her arms over her chest. "And to tell you the truth, I don't particularly want to."

"Wait a sec." Toby shook his head. "If you don't like something, I can respect that. You're entitled to your opinion. But you can't write stuff off if you haven't even tried it."

She wrinkled her nose, a small smile coming to her lips. "I can't?"

"Come on." Toby grabbed her hand and started to drag her toward the Thai booth. "I promise this'll be the best food you've ever tasted."

Fran laughed. "Okay, okay. Just don't make me

use chopsticks," she said. "This girl is hopeless without a fork."

Toby stopped in place and stared right into Fran's eyes. "Ms. Delaney," he said, that now-familiar playful smile on his lips, "I find it hard to believe that you could ever be hopeless at anything."

Toby had said it in a teasing tone, but it somehow felt intense to Fran. Her eyes darted to the grass as her breath caught in her throat. "Thanks," she said softly.

Fran and Toby made their way over to the Thai booth, where Toby ordered the pad thai. They carried their take-out carton and two plastic plates over to a spot on the grass. Toby scooped some pad thai onto a plate and handed it to Fran. "Dig in."

Fran hesitated, eyeing the noodles with suspicion. "Remember," she said, "I'm the one who always eats the same kind of pizza."

Toby laughed. "I know. I let you get away with that because it was our first date. But I honestly think you'll like this, Fran. Trust me."

Fran gazed into Toby's amused eyes. "Okay," she said. "Here goes!"

She took a bite of pad thai, chewing cautiously for a few seconds. The noodles were tossed with crunchy bean sprouts, little pieces of shrimp and peanuts, and a squeeze of fresh lime juice. "You know, it's not bad," she said, reaching down to take another bite.

"Aha!" Toby grinned. "What'd I tell ya?"

Fran smiled as she chewed, entertained that

Toby was so pleased she liked the food. *It's sweet,* she thought. *He doesn't want me to miss out on things, even if it's just food.* Which she would have, she realized, if it hadn't been for Toby's coaxing. Who knew what other types of food were out there for her to try and enjoy?

While they ate, Toby looked over a flyer listing the bands that were playing at the festival. "There's some fun music," he said, giving Fran a sly smile. "You up for some dancing?"

"No way." She shook her head vehemently. "I'm a lousy dancer."

"I absolutely do not believe that," Toby declared. "You're really graceful—I can tell."

Fran ducked her head a little, her hair swinging in front of her face. She'd never liked dancing before—she always felt too self-conscious—but maybe she'd like dancing with Toby. He had gotten her to enjoy Thai food, after all. "I'll be stepping all over your feet," she warned. "Just wait."

"We'll see about that," Toby replied, winking.

They polished off their food and wandered over to the stage. A band was playing music with a fast Latin beat. "Salsa music," Toby said.

"Mmm." Fran smiled. "I'm sure I'll be just wonderful. I can't even dance to *American* music."

"This is American," Toby said, putting an arm firmly around her waist and propelling her closer to the stage. "It's just a little south of the Illinois border."

Fran laughed, and they started to dance. Completely confused, Fran watched other nearby couples, trying to figure out the moves, but she still kept stepping on Toby's feet and bumping into him. "Didn't I tell you I couldn't do this?" she asked.

Toby spun her around. "Don't be so hard on yourself. I've never danced salsa either."

"Then how come you're not stepping on *my* toes?"

"I probably am," he said. "You're just so nervous about stepping on mine that you don't notice." He gave her a quick hug. "Relax, okay? Just have fun with it."

Fran nodded, but it was hard to relax—Toby's hug had left her surprisingly breathless.

As they continued to dance, Toby kept his eyes on hers. He moved easily—not always in time to the beat, but somehow he looked cool anyway. *Because he's just having a good time,* Fran realized as she gradually loosened up a little. *He doesn't care what he looks like.*

The salsa band finished up their set, and Fran and Toby clapped along with everybody else. "Hey—I was just starting to get the hang of that," Fran said.

"So now you get to learn how to polka," Toby told her as the next band started playing. He immediately started stomping his feet to the music, his hands on his hips. "Come on, Fran," he said, grinning. "Dance with me so I don't look like a *total* idiot."

Toby taught her some basic steps. It was easier than salsa, but sillier too, and Fran couldn't stop laughing as they jumped around. "How do you know how to polka?" she asked Toby, wiping the tears of laughter from her eyes.

He shrugged. "Hang out at places like this and you learn all sorts of stuff."

When the polka band finally took a break, they both collapsed onto the grass. "I'm beat," Fran said, leaning back on her elbows, her face tipped to the blue summer sky.

"That was a good workout," Toby agreed. He lay on his side, facing her and shaking his head. "And you said you didn't know how to dance."

Fran glanced down at him. "Well, I don't."

"You do now."

She smiled. "I guess so. Maybe. Thanks for being so patient."

"Don't thank me," Toby responded, pulling at a blade of grass. "You're a natural. You just had to give it a chance—like the pad thai."

Fran sat back up, wrapping her arms around her tucked-up legs and resting one cheek on her knees, thinking over Toby's words. "Do I seem . . . closed-minded?" she asked after a moment. "Like I'm afraid to try stuff?"

"No. I think it's more like you're comfortable being who you are."

Fran bit her lip. "I think I used to be that way," she said. "My life was exactly how I wanted it. But ever since Dad got married again, I—"

She stopped abruptly, cutting herself off. This was the last subject she felt like talking about. She was supposed to be having fun.

Toby sat up straight, pulling his knees into his chest. "You haven't told me much about your step-family," he remarked.

Fran rolled her eyes. "Believe me, you don't want to hear about them."

"Yeah? What's their story?" His eyes were teasing. "Are they aliens from another planet? Wanted by the FBI?"

Fran giggled. "No."

"Maybe I should meet them," Toby suggested, nudging Fran. "Your dad too. You know, make up my own mind."

Fran couldn't hide her surprise. "Really? You want to?"

"Yeah," Toby said.

He was blushing a little, and now she did too. *Meeting my family,* Fran thought. *That definitely points us in the becoming-a-couple direction.*

"I mean, if you want me to," Toby amended.

"I do," she told him, surprised herself at how sure she was of this. "But I'm warning you, they're nuts. It's not going to be fun."

"Right." Toby nodded. "Just like you were going to be such a horrible dancer."

"I'm serious!" Fran laughed. "But you'll see for yourself. Maybe you could come over for dinner some night next week."

"Sounds good," Toby agreed. He stretched his legs out in front of him. "So, are you ready to ride the unicycle?" he asked. "It's back in the van."

Fran shook her head, grinning. "No way."

"Come on. It's easy."

She raised an eyebrow. "Oh? What about that scrape on your nose?"

Toby shrugged it off. "That was a rare accident. Never happens. Well, almost never," he added. "Come on, just try it."

"I tried pad thai and polka," Fran argued. "Isn't that enough for one day?"

"Maybe you're right. We'll save something for next time."

He was sitting close to her now, and they looked right into each other's eyes. Toby's lips were curved in that easy smile Fran was really starting to like.

Then his gaze turned serious for once. "Fran?"

"What?"

"Do you think we could . . ."

He didn't finish the sentence, but she knew what he wanted to ask. She lifted her lips to his.

Fran had never really kissed a guy before. She'd only had quick good-night pecks with guys she'd had a date or two with. *This* was a real kiss. Warm, intense, intoxicating.

Toby's mouth felt wonderful on hers, but after a minute Fran pulled away, just to catch her breath. "Wow," Toby whispered.

"Double wow," she whispered back.

They sat there for a long moment, smiling stupidly at each other. Toby took Fran's hand and squeezed it lightly. Fran's heart felt fluttery.

Maybe's he's not perfect for me, she thought. *But that kiss sure was!*

Seven

FRAN WENT OVER to Caley's that night to compare notes on their dates. "Well, I thought Miles was Mr. Right, but after today, I'm not convinced," Caley said.

It was a warm summer evening, and they were lounging on Caley's deck. "What happened?" Fran asked, reclining the back of her chair. "You didn't have a good time at the movies?"

"Not really. He insisted on seeing a horror flick even after I told him I hate them," Caley answered. "And then he bought his own popcorn without asking me if I wanted anything."

Fran scrunched up her nose. "He sounds totally selfish. You're not going to go out with him again, are you?"

"Don't know and don't care. But enough about him." Caley twisted in her chair to look at Fran. "I *really* like Toby."

Fran blushed with pleasure. "Yeah?"

"Yeah!"

"So do I," Fran admitted. "I didn't see it coming. I mean, I liked him as a friend right away. But now I think I'm kind of falling for him." Her blush deepened. "He wants to meet my family."

"That's awesome," Caley declared, reaching over to give Fran's arm a squeeze. "You guys make a great couple."

A great couple. Fran's heart beat faster. She'd never been part of a couple before. Were she and Toby really on the verge of becoming boyfriend and girlfriend?

The prospect was exciting, but now that she'd gotten a little distance from her day with Toby, something about it didn't feel quite right. Ever since she'd met Toby, she'd thought about him a lot, but she'd never stopped fantasizing about Museum Guy. He was still her ideal.

"The thing is, Toby and I are pretty different," Fran pointed out, for her own benefit as much as for Caley's. "Like, he's totally outgoing and I'm quiet. He's quirky and offbeat; I'm pretty mainstream. I want to be a museum curator; he's a juggler. See what I'm saying?"

Caley shook her head. "No. Being different can be a plus, Franny. The way I see it, you two complement each other." She let out a sigh. "And if you're saying all this because you're still pining over Museum Guy, forget about it. Whoever he is, he can't be half as cool as Toby."

Caley hopped to her feet. "I'm going inside to grab a soda. Want one?"

"No, thanks," Fran said, musing over Caley's words as she walked away.

Was Caley right? Did she and Toby complement each other? From the start, Fran had thought Toby was interesting and funny and even kind of cute, but she also thought he was a little off the wall. She hadn't expected to end up liking him, but now there was no denying the signs. So she didn't dissolve into jelly around him the way she did whenever she spotted Museum Guy, but she did get warm inside, and she thought about him a lot, and she could hardly wait until she saw him again.

Besides, Fran told herself, *Museum Guy might be your ideal, but what are the odds that you'll ever even talk to him? Toby's the one you're hanging out with and really getting to know.*

It's just like Caley said, she thought as she gazed up into the darkening sky. *Go for it with the real guy instead of pining after the fantasy one . . . because Museum Guy's definitely nothing but a fantasy.*

At drawing class on Monday, Fran was proud of herself for taking an easel a couple of places away from Museum Guy even though the one right next to his was still vacant . . . but not for long. Audrey—the pretty black-haired girl—slipped right into the space.

Audrey and Museum Guy started chatting in a familiar way, and Fran immediately felt a surge of jealousy. *I don't care if they flirt all night,* she reminded herself as she watched them out of the corner of her eye. Still, she couldn't help pushing her hair behind her ear to try to hear a little bit of their conversation. They were talking about which brand of charcoal pencil they liked best—not that hot a topic, Fran was relieved to discover.

Not that I really care or anything, she told herself.

Brigitte and the model strolled into the studio, and class got started. *Just focus on your drawing. Don't think about him,* she reminded herself for the tenth time. *Toby's coming over tomorrow night. Think about that instead.*

She tried to think about Toby and focus on her artwork, but every few minutes her attention—and her eyes—strayed. That night Museum Guy was wearing faded jeans and a T-shirt with ripped-off sleeves. As he sketched, the muscles in his right arm flexed impressively. His jaw was clenched from concentration, making his profile look more sculpted than ever, and now and then he flicked his hair back from his face by jerking his head in a way Fran found wildly attractive.

She fanned her warm cheeks with a piece of sketch paper. *Don't look,* she instructed herself, and for ten whole minutes she didn't. She didn't need to, because now her imagination had taken over. In this particular fantasy, she and Museum Guy had left the art supplies at home for once. They were on the beach, and he'd taken off his T-shirt so she could rub suntan lotion into those incredible shoulders. . . .

Fran shook her head. *What is it about him?* she wondered, a bit desperately. Her daydreams about him were always so intensely romantic, so much more compelling than her moments with Toby. *What does that say about Toby and me? What's missing with us?*

★　　★　　★

65

Fran glanced around the dining room table, wondering if she'd entered the Twilight Zone. She was having dinner with Toby and her family, all stepsiblings present and accounted for, and she was actually *enjoying* herself.

Okay, so she'd been completely annoyed at first when Drea bombarded Toby with a million questions and the twins shoveled their food into their mouths as if they didn't know that such a thing as table manners existed. But Toby had been so patient and charming with them that he somehow made *them* seem sort of charming. For the first time since her father had married Emma, Fran actually regarded her younger siblings as being sort of . . . *cute*.

At the moment Toby and Drea were having a heated discussion about the TV show *Malibu Heights*. Fran didn't know what shocked her more: the fact that Toby actually watched that trash or the way that Drea was blossoming under his attention. Her brown eyes sparkled as she spoke to him, and she giggled incessantly.

Who knew there was such an unbratty side to her? Fran thought in wonder as she watched.

Toby hit it off with the twins too. Douglas and William had gotten into their own conversation about a movie they'd just seen, called *Doomsday on Planet Z*.

"Hey, yeah," Toby cut in, switching his attention over to them. "Wasn't it cool when the mobile alien command center thing collided with that space probe from Earth and there were alien body parts flying all over the place?"

The twins' heads swiveled in tandem as they turned to stare at Toby. Fran stared too. "You saw *Planet Z*?" Douglas asked, his hazel eyes growing wide.

Toby nodded. "Twice. I got my cousin some of the action figures, though, and he said they were lame."

"The action figures are definitely lame," William confirmed. "But the video game is awesome."

Fran smiled to herself at the solemn tone in which her little brother spoke about this subject. Emma caught her eye across the table and winked.

Toby should come over more often, Fran thought, standing up to help clear the table. *Then maybe my family life would be more bearable.*

After they'd all cleaned up, Fran and Toby walked out to the porch so that they could be alone for a little while. They sat in the hammock together in the twilight, swinging and talking.

"I can't get over it," Fran told him. "You were amazing with them—they were amazing with you. There's got to be something you're not telling me. Are you sure you don't have any younger brothers and sisters?"

Toby laughed. "I swear I'm not keeping any deep, dark secrets. I only have one older brother, Marshall."

"So what's the trick?"

"No trick. I'm just interested in people."

"Even little kids?" Fran asked.

"Sure." Toby smiled. "Don't forget that I'm a camp counselor." He ran a hand through his hair. "Kids have their own unique world. You just have to get into it."

"Sorry, but Douglas and William's world is

absolutely the last place I want to be," Fran said. "I'd rather live on Planet Z!"

Toby put an arm around her and gave her a little squeeze. "Well, I for one am glad you don't live on another planet."

Fran laughed. "Thanks."

"Anytime," he teased. "I guess the hard part of the blended-family thing is that you didn't grow up with them," he speculated. "They just appeared."

"Maybe that's it," Fran agreed. She let out a sigh. "I don't know. Sometimes I think if there were only one of them, maybe I could deal with it. But I just feel like they crowd me out."

"Because you're used to being an only child, right?"

"Yes." Fran nodded. "I guess so."

"Well, you'll think I'm nuts," Toby began, "but I'm kind of envious. I think it would be cool to have a lot of siblings. I just have Marsh, and we're not that tight."

"How come?" she asked, surprised. It seemed as though Toby could get along with just about anybody.

He shook his head. "Don't know. It's not that we don't have anything in common. We're both into art. But I guess it takes two people to have a good relationship, and Marsh is kind of . . . self-involved. Off in his own world or something."

Toby shifted positions, and Fran slid closer to him on the hammock. Now he had both his arms wrapped around her, and a rush of warmth spread throughout her body. "Sounds to me like it's Marshall's loss," she said softly.

"That's what I think, of course," Toby joked.

Fran pulled back a little to smile up at him, and as she did he leaned down to kiss her.

It was just as she'd remembered—warm, soft . . . and perfect. She didn't want the kiss ever to end.

When it did, Toby brushed a stray wisp of hair back from her forehead with his finger. "I really like you, Fran," he said.

She gazed at him, her heart beating fast. "I really like you too."

"I mean, I'm falling for you. Hard." His eyes crinkled, as if they were smiling. "I can't believe I found you that day by the lake. Is it fate or what?"

Too overwhelmed to speak, Fran simply pressed her cheek against Toby's shoulder and nodded.

She hadn't been looking for a boyfriend that summer, and Toby wasn't necessarily the one she'd have picked for herself. Up until that evening, she'd still been comparing him to Museum Guy, and Toby hadn't always measured up. But suddenly everything looked different to her. *I feel at home in his arms,* she thought. *I want to stay here a long, long time.*

Lifting her face, she kissed Toby again. *He's the one,* she thought, feeling floaty and light-headed with happiness. Toby made her laugh—even around her family. He got her to try new things. She liked being with him more than anyone. On top of all that, it turned out he was a *great* kisser.

And summer's more than half over, Fran realized. Now that she'd found Toby, she didn't plan to waste a minute more thinking about that other guy.

Eight

TWO MORNINGS LATER Fran walked across the Northwestern campus, heading for the art history building. It was a sunny, breezy day, and for the first time since she'd started assisting Professor Baird, she seriously wished she worked someplace else.

Fran took a sniff as she stepped into the office. It had a musty, too-many-books-and-not-enough-windows smell. "Morning, Professor Baird," she said.

He looked up from his desk, adjusting his bifocals. He was about sixty and had fluffy white Albert Einstein hair. "Morning, Frances. I have a pile of slides for you to sort and catalog on the computer. Do you want to get a cup of coffee from the faculty lounge first?"

"No, thanks," Fran told him. "I'll just get started."

Fran settled down at a worktable in the corner of the office and began shuffling through the slides: Dutch and Flemish, Renaissance Italian, rococo, sixteenth-century Japanese, French Impressionist. She yawned.

At some point Professor Baird had trotted off to the library. Now, cupping her chin in her hand, Fran gazed out the window.

This dim office was good for one thing . . . daydreaming. And luckily Fran had other things to think about than who came first, Rembrandt or El Greco. In the past, she'd fantasized about Museum Guy, but that morning she closed her eyes and relived those magical kisses with Toby on the hammock a few nights earlier. *And tonight I'm going to meet* his *family,* she thought, excited.

When her three hours for Professor Baird were up, Fran took the bus into the city. Walking up the steps to the Art Institute, she couldn't help wondering—as she always did—if she'd run into Museum Guy. *Not that I* want *to,* she thought.

But there he was, as gorgeous as ever, saying something to a tour group that was about to start.

Fran watched as he led the group off. She didn't follow them, but she did feel a moment of sadness, almost like saying good-bye. She'd dreamed about Museum Guy for half the summer. But she didn't need fantasy anymore. Real life was better.

And I don't have any regrets, Fran thought, heading purposefully in the opposite direction with her sketch pad.

Fran borrowed her dad's car to drive over to the Kalbhens'. Toby lived in a green frame house with a big stone porch, and every square foot of the small front yard was planted with flowering shrubs.

Toby's parents had to be the friendliest people in the world. They both came to the door when Fran rang the bell.

"Fran Delaney," Mr. Kalbhen boomed immediately. Seizing Fran's hand, he gave it a vigorous shake. He looked a little like a younger, blond-haired Santa Claus, and when he smiled, his blue eyes practically disappeared in the crinkles. "Let me tell you, Toby has a lot of friends, but lately you're the only one he talks about."

Toby stood in the hall behind his parents. "*Dad,*" he groaned.

Toby's mother stepped forward and gave Fran a quick hug. She was blond and jolly-looking as well. "Come on in, Fran," she invited with a warm smile. "Do you like burgers and potato salad?" A bit overwhelmed, Fran just nodded. "Great!" Mrs. Kalbhen exclaimed. "Why don't you and Toby come with me into the kitchen? I could use some help while Hal grills."

Toby caught her eye and winked at her. She smiled. "Sure," she said. "Of course."

In the kitchen, Toby and Fran sliced carrots and cucumbers while Mrs. Kalbhen made salad dressing. "Is Marsh around?" Toby asked his mother.

"No," she answered, splashing vinegar into a small mixing bowl. She turned to Fran. "We're not necessarily expecting Marshall in time for dinner. He knows you're coming over, but . . ." She shrugged.

"He's nineteen, and college kids develop very independent habits."

"That's a nice way of putting it," Toby teased.

Mrs. Kalbhen shook her head. "You'll be there yourself in a few years, Tobias."

Toby's mom crossed the kitchen to the pantry. "Tobias?" Fran whispered to Toby, trying not to giggle. "What kind of name is that?"

He put down his knife so that he could slip an arm around her and tickle her waist. "I don't know, *Frances,*" he whispered back.

Back at her mixing bowl, Mrs. Kalbhen energetically whisked the salad dressing. "Fran, Toby told me you're working for an art history professor at Northwestern this summer," she remarked.

"Yes." Fran quickly straightened her shirt, which Toby had rumpled. "Just part-time. The rest of the time I go to the Art Institute to sketch and stuff."

"That's a coincidence," Mrs. Kalbhen said. "Has Toby told you that Marshall—"

Just then the timer on the stove went off. Mrs. Kalbhen scooped Toby and Fran's cucumber and carrot slices into the wooden salad bowl, then stepped over to the oven to switch the buzzer off. "Time to take the burgers off the grill, Hal," she called. "Toby, would you put the salad on the table? I think we should just go ahead and eat." She gave Fran an apologetic smile. "Usually Marshall at least calls if he's not going to be home for dinner, but you just never know with him."

Fran helped Toby carry food to the table, and a

73

moment later Mr. Kalbhen walked in with the platter of hamburgers.

"What were you starting to say before about Marshall?" Fran asked Mrs. Kalbhen.

The front door slammed, making them all jump. "That he goes to the Art Institute as well," Mrs. Kalbhen said. "But it sounds like Marshall made it home after all. He can tell you himself." Twisting in her chair, she called, "Come on into the dining room, Marsh. Dinner's ready."

Toby nudged her foot under the table, smiling. "You'll meet the whole family after all," he told her. "Marsh is the last piece of the mysterious puzzle of my personality."

Mr. and Mrs. Kalbhen began to pass serving bowls. As Fran spooned some potato salad onto her plate, she looked over at the dining room entrance.

And she almost fainted.

A tall, well-built guy with longish golden hair and intense blue eyes had stepped into view. "Sorry I'm late, Mom," he said in a deep voice. He smiled, his gaze moving to Fran. "Hope I didn't miss the party."

Fran's heart beat wildly. Her palms began to sweat. *Wh-What's Museum Guy doing here?* she wondered crazily, her stomach doing cartwheels.

Then it hit her. Fran could've sworn that she'd stopped breathing altogether.

Museum Guy was Toby's brother! Marshall was Museum Guy!

Her mouth fell open and she snapped it shut,

simultaneously dropping both the bowl she was holding and the serving spoon. There was a clatter of china as potato salad splattered all over the tablecloth. Fran didn't even notice. She was still gaping at Marshall.

It can't be him, she thought, her mind numb with shock. Was this one of her old fantasies come to life with a perverse, sickening twist?

But it *was* him.

He was standing there in the flesh—the incomparably gorgeous flesh—watching her with an amused smile on his handsome face.

"Oops!" Mrs. Kalbhen said. "Here, let me help clean that up."

"Are you all right?" Toby asked Fran. "You look like you just saw a ghost."

Fran came to with a start. *Oh, my God. Museum Guy is Marshall,* she thought, her brain spinning like mad. *My boyfriend's older brother. Oh, my God.*

"I'm fine," she assured Toby. "I've got it, Mrs. Kalbhen." Hastily trying to scoop the potato salad back into the bowl, she knocked over her water glass. Fran was sure that her face, which had definitely been pink before, now must have been positively fuchsia.

"I'm such a klutz," she muttered, wishing there were some way she could magically transport herself out of this moment. She knew that Museum Guy—rather, Marshall—was still watching her. Everyone was watching her at this point. *And if my face gets any hotter,* Fran thought, *I'll catch fire.*

"Don't worry about it," Toby said, mopping up

the spilled water with his napkin. "Hey, relax, okay?" He put an arm around her and gave her a playful squeeze. "I know he looks scary and everything, but he doesn't bite."

"Usually," Marshall added in the deep, entrancing voice Fran knew only too well.

Fran took a shaky breath, struggling to compose herself. At least Toby's parents had gone into the kitchen to get Marshall a place setting and to bring some fresh potato salad to the table. Maybe she could calm herself down before they returned.

Relax, like Toby said, Fran ordered herself. *Try to act normal.*

But it was impossible. How could she act normal when the guy she'd been panting over all summer had turned up in her boyfriend's house . . . and turned out to be her boyfriend's *brother?* The very last person on the planet she'd have wanted Museum Guy to be, just when she'd determined never to think or dream about him again?

Maybe he'll take off again, Fran hoped silently. From the way Toby and his parents talked about him, Fran had gotten the impression Marshall had a pretty active social life. *Please let him have a date . . . even with Audrey from drawing class!*

Instead, Marshall lifted his chin at his younger brother. "Hey, Toby," he said. "Aren't you going to introduce me?"

"Yeah, of course," Toby answered. "I'd just forgotten in all the commotion. Fran, this is Marshall. Marsh, Fran Delaney."

Marshall came around the table to shake her hand. As Fran stood up she bumped into her chair, knocking it into the wall behind her. That wasn't all that was knocking either. Underneath her long rayon skirt, her knees were jiggling like Jell-O.

"Nice to meet you," Marshall said as he reached for her hand. His eyes stayed fixed on hers. Their fingers touched, and there was a spark. Fran jumped.

"Sorry." Marshall smiled. "Must've rubbed my shoes on the carpet."

"That's okay," Fran said, fairly certain she was about to spontaneously combust.

Marshall didn't let go of her hand right away, and Fran felt herself growing warmer and warmer, if that was possible.

I can't believe this is happening, she thought, delirious now from shock *and* from the touch of Museum Guy's hand. *I'm finally meeting him!*

Marshall narrowed his eyes at her. "Hope this doesn't sound like a line," he said to Fran, dropping her hand, "but haven't I met you somewhere?"

"Um . . . maybe you've seen me at the museum," she mumbled. "I hang out there a lot." *And I've been putting a lot of energy into spying on you!* "Also, I, uh, think we're in the same drawing class on Monday nights."

Marshall snapped his fingers. "Yep. That's it. I've definitely noticed you."

Mr. and Mrs. Kalbhen returned to the table, Marshall sat down, and Fran sank back into her own chair. *He's noticed me!* was all she could think, thrilled to the core.

"You're taking that drawing class too?" Toby asked Marshall.

Fran looked at her boyfriend. In her shock and inner tumult over Marshall, she'd almost forgotten that Toby was sitting right next to her.

Marshall nodded. "Yeah. It was kind of a last-minute move. I've been blowing it off, actually."

"Marshall's a tour guide at the Art Institute," Mrs. Kalbhen told Fran.

"I know," Fran said, managing to keep her voice relatively even. She shot a glance at Marshall. "I mean, I think maybe I've seen you there."

"It's not a bad summer job." Marshall gave her a wink. "Buys the beer, you know?"

"I hope not," Mr. Kalbhen said.

"Just kidding, Dad."

Everybody went on eating and chatting. For Fran, though, the rest of the meal was a blur. She couldn't eat more than a bite or two—she was afraid she'd knock her glass over again or do something worse. Her whole body was tingling in a completely disconcerting way, and not because Toby kept playing footsie with her. Museum Guy was sitting right across the table!

I have to stop thinking about him like that, Fran thought. *He's Marshall, Toby's brother. I have to forget about ever having had a huge crush on him.* But how could she when her crazy attraction was back full force?

78

When dinner was over, Marshall stood up. "Sorry to eat and run, but I'm meeting somebody. And Fran . . ." Those incredible eyes moved to her face. Fran's pulse quickened to warp speed. "Pleasure meeting you."

"Same," she said, her voice little more than a squeak.

"I'll look for you at the museum," he said, still gazing right at her.

The museum. The place where it had all started. She felt herself flush with excitement despite all her efforts to stay cool and casual. "Great," she said, still squeaking.

Marshall's eyes shifted to Toby, and he gave his brother a rakish wink. "Have fun, bro. Don't do anything I wouldn't do."

"Later, dude," Toby said.

Toby insisted on driving home with Fran that night, his ten-speed bike in the Pontiac's backseat. Marshall might as well have been in the backseat too, considering how intensely Fran still felt his presence. Toby was gabbing about stuff he wanted to do together. Fortunately, he didn't seem to have any idea that Fran was answering in monosyllables because she was totally preoccupied with his brother.

I just can't believe it, she thought as she pulled the car into her driveway. It was the hugest, craziest coincidence. Her dream guy, the biggest crush of her whole life, was Toby's older brother.

My former dream guy, Fran corrected herself. *My ex-crush. Everything changed when I met Toby.*

79

Or had it?

She turned off the car's engine. Toby took off his seat belt. Mechanically Fran did the same. When Toby wrapped his arms around her, though, she couldn't respond with any real warmth.

"What did you think of my parents?" Toby asked.

"They're great," Fran said.

"They're decent," he agreed. "Marsh isn't a bad guy either."

"He's nice," Fran said, trying her best to sound neutral.

"Well, he has good taste, at least," Toby said. "I could tell he approved of you. Which is kind of important, because even though we don't see eye to eye on a lot of stuff, I respect his opinion. And . . ." Toby shifted in the passenger seat so he could look into Fran's eyes. His voice grew husky. "I want my whole family to like the girl I'm falling in love with."

Love. It was the first time either of them had used the L word. Fran blinked at Toby in surprise, momentarily forgetting all about Marshall.

"I hope it's okay I said that," Toby added quickly. "I don't mean to rush things."

"It's all right." Fran gazed into Toby's warm eyes and, like a landslide, all her feelings for him came rushing back. "I think I'm falling in love with you too," she whispered.

Toby's arms tightened around her. He bent down and kissed her, and it was more passionate and more intense than any kiss they'd shared before.

For five whole minutes, while she and Toby

prolonged their goodnight, Fran didn't think about her boyfriend's brother. It was so sweet to be together like this, so amazing to hear Toby say "I love you" for the first time, so earthshaking to say it back.

But after Toby had sped off down the quiet street and she was alone in her house, Fran dropped down from cloud nine with a thump.

In her moonlit room, with Drea breathing softly in the far bed, Fran stood in front of the shadowy mirror and stared at her own reflection. "I'm in love with Toby," she whispered to the mirror. "I *am*." But then why was her heart pounding not from the memory of Toby's kisses, but at the thought that the next day she might run into Marshall at the Art Institute?

Is Marshall the guy for me, or is Toby? Fran wondered. She didn't know a lot about love, but she was sure about one thing: They couldn't *both* be.

Nine

"**Y**OU'RE KIDDING!" CALEY exclaimed.

"Shh," Fran hissed.

They were on the downtown bus the next morning, and Fran had just told Caley about the previous night's shocker.

"Museum Guy is Toby's brother," Caley said, her voice only slightly lower. "You're *kidding!*"

"I wish I was." Fran chewed on her fingernails. "Then maybe I wouldn't have had the dream I had last night."

"What'd you dream about?"

Fran shook her head, blushing at the memory. "I can't go into details. Let's just say it was pretty steamy and it wasn't about Toby."

The bus reached Caley's stop. Caley jumped up, grabbing Fran's hand. "Come on," she said. "Get off here with me. I don't have to be at my desk for"—she checked her watch—"twelve minutes. We can

82

get a cup of coffee and you can tell me more."

Obediently Fran followed Caley into the coffee shop down the block from Caley's office. They ordered coffee and a blueberry muffin to share.

"I was really ready to write off this crush," Fran told Caley. "Seriously. I knew nothing would ever come of it, and now I have a relationship with Toby and it's amazing. But last night . . ." She felt herself turn crimson again, remembering how she'd reacted when Marshall took her hand and said he'd noticed her at the museum. "I feel so guilty, Caley. I think I'm in love with Toby, but I'm crushing worse than ever on his brother."

"This is too wild," Caley said, breaking the muffin in half and handing Fran her portion. "It's like you're living a real-life soap!"

"I do *not* want this to turn into a soap," Fran said.

"It doesn't have to," Caley assured her, popping a piece of muffin into her mouth. "Take me and Miles. Remember how I was ninety-nine percent sure he and I were meant to be?"

"Ninety-nine point nine percent."

"Exactly. And where is Miles now?"

"On his bike delivering packages?" Fran guessed.

"History. Miles is history." Caley sniffed in disgust. "He turned out to be a total dud."

"How does this relate to me?" Fran asked.

"My point is, now that you know who Museum Guy is, he's not a mystery anymore. Doesn't that make him a little less fascinating?"

Fran thought about this for a moment. Sure, the

83

mystery had been part of the attraction. But her old crush on Museum Guy was nowhere near as strong as her new and improved crush on Marshall Kalbhen—the guy who'd looked straight into her eyes, spoken her name, and promised to look out for her at the museum.

"No," Fran admitted helplessly. "It doesn't."

"Well, it had better," Caley said, "or you're doomed. Falling in love with your boyfriend's brother is, like, the biggest no-no."

Fran couldn't eat her half of the blueberry muffin—she felt sick to her stomach—so she handed it back to Caley. "I haven't fallen in love with him," she said, which was true. She'd *imagined* falling in love with him, though, many, many times.

"It would be a different story if he were somebody else," Caley said, eating the rest of the muffin. "Anybody else. Then I'd say sure, pursue it a little. Why not? But now that you know he's Toby's brother, you've got to nip this crush in the bud. Or you'll lose Toby."

Fran's fingers tightened around her coffee cup. "I don't want to lose Toby," she whispered.

"I know."

They silently finished their coffee and left it at that. Caley went to work and Fran hopped back on the bus, continuing downtown toward the Art Institute.

I don't want to lose Toby, I don't want to lose Toby, she chanted silently to the hum of the bus's engine. *I'll stop crushing on Marshall, I'll stop crushing on Marshall.*

Maybe that was all there was to it. *Mind over matter, right?* she thought optimistically. *I'm strong. I'll need to be.*

Inside the museum, Fran headed to a section she rarely visited: European decorative arts and sculpture. *I'll never run into Marshall down here,* she thought as she studied the suits of armor and ornate antique furnishings, looking for something to sketch. She decided on an intricately painted ceramic wine cistern from sixteenth-century Italy, then settled onto a bench close by. A couple of weeks of sleuthing had shown her that when Marshall drew on his own, he preferred paintings to sculpture.

So when he walked into the room five minutes later, Fran dropped her pencil and her sketch pad as well.

Her pulse racing, she quickly picked up her things, then watched Marshall as he stopped in front of a glass display case, telling his tour group about the suit of armor inside.

Then he spotted Fran. His blue eyes brightened with recognition. "Excuse me for a moment," he said to the group, stepping over to her. "Hey, Fran."

"H-Hi. I didn't think you were working today," she stammered.

"I'm subbing for someone." Marshall glanced at the tourists, then tapped his wristwatch. "Will you still be around in an hour and a half?"

Fran nodded, speechless.

"I'll look for you," he said. "Upstairs by *La Grande Jatte*."

And with that, Marshall moved off with his group.

Fran caught her breath, exhaling slowly. Then she tried to concentrate on her drawing of the wine cistern, but it was useless.

I should have stayed home today, Fran thought guiltily. What if for some reason Toby came by the museum and saw her with his brother?

But we aren't doing anything wrong, she reminded herself. She and Marshall were going to meet by a big painting and maybe talk for a few minutes. They were just being friendly. Toby would expect them to do that, wouldn't he? Besides, nothing was going to happen. She might be attracted to Marshall, but he wasn't attracted to *her*. No way.

For some reason, that thought didn't completely ease Fran's feelings of guilt. She tapped her pencil on the paper, her forehead creased with worry.

Nothing good's going to come of this, she couldn't help thinking as a pit formed in her stomach.

An hour later Fran went upstairs to where Seurat's famous painting was displayed. As she approached *La Grande Jatte,* Marshall walked across the gallery from the opposite direction. Fran tried not to hyperventilate over the fact that this amazing-looking older guy was heading straight for *her*.

"I only have half an hour," Marshall told Fran when he reached her. "Wanna grab a quick bite to eat?"

He only has half an hour and he wants to spend

it with me! Fran thought, flattered and excited despite all her best intentions. "Sure," she said.

They bought sandwiches at the café and took them outside to the park next to the museum. "What a day," Marshall commented, sitting down on the grass and leaning back on his elbows. Sun glinted on his golden hair. "Almost makes me wish I were a lifeguard or something."

"Really?" Fran asked, surprised.

He sat up straight and grinned, holding Fran's gaze for a prolonged moment. "I said *almost.*"

"Right." Fran smiled slightly, her eyes nervously darting to the ground. *After all those weeks of fantasizing, I'm actually having lunch with him,* she thought as she unwrapped her sandwich. *Him and me. Me and him.*

"I've read your dad's textbook, did I tell you that?" Marshall asked, taking a bite of his own sandwich.

Fran looked back up at him. "You have?"

"It was pretty much the bible in the art history class I took last semester at Michigan," Marshall told her. "The first and last word."

"Well . . . cool," she said, feeling absurdly pleased.

"Despite the tour guide gig, though, I don't know if I'm cut out to be a scholar myself." Marshall's eyes shone with unbelievable intensity as he spoke. A red-hot shiver traveled down her spine. "I'm more physical than cerebral," he continued. "I love the feeling of the brush in my hand, the sensuality of applying paint to canvas. I need to create with all of me. Know what I mean?"

"Yes," she squeaked.

"So . . ." Marshall's lips formed into a slow half smile. Actually, it was kind of like Toby's smile . . . except it was sexier. "You're dating my baby brother."

"Well, we just started, you know, going out." When she heard herself babble on, Fran wished she could disappear. "But . . . yeah."

"He's a nice kid."

It was an offhand remark and not exactly a compliment. He made Toby sound too young to count. *What about me?* Fran wondered. *Does Marshall think I'm just a "nice kid" too?*

"He's got some crazy ideas, though," Marshall went on. "Like this art-for-inner-city-kids thing. Has he talked to you about that?"

Fran nodded. "It sounds pretty ambitious."

"It'll never get off the ground," Marshall predicted. "He has no clue how hard the organizing part would be. And also, you can't throw people together who have nothing in common and expect them to click, or take kids who've had zero exposure to art and expect them to instantly discover some great hidden talent." He gulped down some of his soda. "It's classic Toby, though—he's all over the place. In my opinion, a person is either an artist or a social worker. You can't be both."

When Toby had first told her his idea, Fran had a doubt or two as well. But she thought Toby's sincerity should count for something. Marshall didn't seem to give his younger brother any credit at all. "Toby thinks people from different backgrounds *can* find common ground and become friends," Fran said.

"Yeah, well, Toby's a dreamer," Marshall said dismissively.

"Isn't everybody who tries to start something new?"

"Maybe. Anyway, it's his head. He can bang it against the wall all he wants to."

It didn't seem fair that Toby wasn't there to defend himself, so Fran was prepared to argue a little more. But Marshall was looking at his watch. "I have to go lead a tour," he said.

They gathered up their lunch stuff and stood up. "And I've got to catch a bus," Fran told him.

Marshall smiled. "Well, it was nice talking to you."

He did that eye contact thing again, gazing at Fran until she had to look down. "You too," she said. "So long."

"See you in drawing class Monday night."

"Right—drawing class." Anticipating it, Fran felt warm all over. This time she'd stroll across the studio and take the easel right next to Marshall's. *Move over, Audrey!* she thought.

As Fran climbed on the northbound bus a few minutes later, she conducted a silent inner debate. *We ate lunch together, but it was totally innocent,* she reasoned. *I'm just trying to get to know my boyfriend's brother. Nothing wrong with that . . . is there?*

The bus turned onto Lake Shore Drive, and Fran stared out the window at the lake. If having lunch with Marshall was so harmless, why was she feeling so guilty about it? Maybe because from up close, he was even more gorgeous than she'd thought before. Maybe because every time he looked at her, the sparks practically set her on fire. So much for losing interest in him just because the mystery was gone!

Fran recalled her plan at the beginning of the day: to steer clear of Marshall so that her crush would safely fade away. But Marshall was Toby's brother. She couldn't totally avoid him even if she wanted to.

We're bound to see each other around, Fran thought. *But maybe if I make some ground rules for myself, like if I just talk with him about impersonal stuff, I won't have to feel guilty.*

Yes, that's it, she decided, relieved that she'd figured things out. *We can talk—but only small talk. That's where I'll draw the line.*

Late Sunday afternoon Fran met Toby for a bike/unicycle ride along the shore. After they'd gone a couple of miles, they parked their wheels and sat in the dunes, looking out toward the water.

"Hey, guess what?" Toby asked.

"What?"

"I have good news about the arts outreach project." He took Fran's hand and gave her fingers an excited squeeze. "It's gonna happen! I'll be able to get it started this fall, as soon as school starts again."

The broad smile on Toby's face was as bright as the sun. Fran felt a surge of affection and pride. "That's awesome!" she cried, flinging her arms around him.

"Now comes the hard part," Toby went on. "I need to call a bunch of teachers and see if I can find an adviser, and then I need to recruit student volunteers—a bunch of them."

"You can do it," Fran assured him.

"Well . . . how about you?" Toby looked at her with a hopeful expression. "I'd love us to work together on this."

"Oh." Fran's smile faded as she tried to picture herself talking about oils and acrylics with some inner-city kid. She hated letting Toby down, but she had to be honest about her feelings. "You know, I really don't think I'm cut out for that kind of thing."

"Why not?"

She looked away, scooping up a handful of sand and letting the grains sift through her fingers. "It's just not my personality. I'm not outgoing enough. I'm into art, not social work."

Toby flopped back on the sand, his arms folded behind his head. "That sounds like something Marsh would say."

Fran wrinkled her nose. "Does it?" Then she remembered that Marshall *had* said something like that the other day.

Fran blushed, feeling as though she'd been caught at something. *Did Marshall mention our little lunch to Toby?* she wondered, suddenly nervous. "Um . . . I wouldn't know," she mumbled.

"Marshall has these theories about the relationship between life and art," Toby explained. "As if the people who make and appreciate art are this rare breed, separate from the rest of us cretins." He rolled over on the sand and looked at Fran. "I don't buy that. I think the best art comes when you're involved with the world around you."

"I know you believe that," she said, nodding, "and that's how you live." She gazed out to the horizon, thinking of all the countless magical hours she'd spent at the Art Institute. "What I love about art, though, is that it *is* separate from real life. It's a world apart. It's . . . purer or something."

"Well, it's okay with me if we agree to disagree on this. I won't bug you anymore about volunteering." He pushed Fran's hair away from her face, giving her a mischievous smile. "For now. I'll win you over to my side eventually."

Toby's hand moved from her hair to her shoulder. Fran reached out to hug him, grateful that he was so understanding.

Their arms around each other, they fell back lightly onto the sand. It was a warm, intimate moment, and Fran felt incredibly close to Toby—closer than she ever had before. "I'm crazy about you, Fran," he whispered into her hair. "I can't think about anything else."

She closed her eyes, wishing she could say the same thing, but it wouldn't have been quite true. When Toby started kissing her, she almost forgot about Marshall.

Almost.

Ten

MONDAY WAS ONE of those rainy midsummer Chicago days when it felt more like winter than summer. And it couldn't have been a worse day for Fran. After putting in her boring hours at Professor Baird's, she ran all the way home from the bus stop, but still got completely drenched.

Then she discovered that Douglas and William had been using her pastels, brushes, and paints for some idiotic art project they'd concocted, nearly ruining all of her supplies. She yelled at them, but they didn't seem to realize that they'd done anything wrong.

Fran thought her afternoon couldn't get much worse, but it did. When Emma got home, Fran expected some vindication, but her stepmother barely even punished the twins. And when Fran accused Emma of being unfair, her dad sprang to his wife's defense.

Forget this family, Fran seethed as she got into the car to drive to painting class that evening. *I don't fit in, and I don't need them. They just drive me nuts.*

But halfway to the Art Institute, an amazing thing happened as Fran's thoughts drifted to her upcoming class. First her mood mellowed a little bit, and then she got downright giddy. A song she liked came on the radio, and she cranked the volume, singing along.

I'm just psyched to get out of the house, she told herself. *My mood doesn't have anything to do with Marshall.* After all, she had a wonderful, one-in-a-million boyfriend. She was in love for the first time in her life, and it was new and exciting and important, and she'd never jeopardize Toby's trust by being disloyal to him in any way.

But when she got to the studio, Marshall greeted her with a heart-stopping smile. "Saved you an easel," he said.

Suddenly Fran couldn't pretend anymore. Marshall was the reason she'd taken the class in the first place— and now her dream of talking to him and having the easel next to his had come true. And, disproving Caley's theory, the more Fran got to know him, the more attracted to him she became.

The class was doing ten-minute poses, and that night Fran drew with uncharacteristic passion. Being so near to Marshall charged her with an energy that seemed to flow straight from her body onto the paper.

When the model took a break, Marshall looked

at Fran's most recent sketch. "Wow," he said.

Fran blushed. Her drawings were okay, but nowhere near as good as Marshall's. "I didn't get the arms right."

"Are you kidding? The figure looks coiled up and ready to spring. You totally captured it."

Fran's blush deepened. He couldn't know how incredibly thrilled his praise made her. "Thanks."

"We've got ten minutes." Marshall nodded toward the door. "Want to duck outside and get some fresh air?"

This was the kind of situation Fran had promised herself she'd avoid, but at the moment her willpower was nonexistent. "Okay," she said.

They walked along the sidewalk outside the museum. The sun had just set and the rain had ended, leaving behind a purple-and-orange sky. Fran couldn't help thinking that Marshall looked especially gorgeous and romantic against this dramatic backdrop.

"You seemed frazzled when you came in tonight," Marshall commented, glancing over at her.

"I was. I had a fight with my dad and stepmom," she explained. "My stepbrothers raided my closet and basically ruined all my art stuff. Maybe I did make too big a deal about it, but sometimes I really want to strangle those guys."

"Families are more trouble than they're worth," Marshall said. "I mean, my parents are pretty harmless. But just because you're related to people doesn't mean you have anything in common with them."

"That's true. And I'm not even related to Douglas and William, or their mom."

He shrugged. "My advice is, get a lock for your closet door and then just keep clear of the whole crew."

Marshall grinned at her, and Fran couldn't help smiling back. "Believe me, I've thought about moving into the museum," she joked.

"I'll keep my eyes open for a place for you to hide."

A heavy, loaded silence fell between them as they continued to smile at each other. Suddenly feeling guilty, Fran brought up her boyfriend. "Isn't it cool that Toby's outreach program is going to work out?" she asked quickly.

"Mmm." Fran took this for an affirmative answer. Marshall didn't pursue the topic, though. "Speaking of my bro, how'd you meet Toby anyway?"

"Oh," she said. "Well, I was at the beach one afternoon sketching, and he was on his unicycle. Juggling," she added lamely, aware of how ridiculous this sounded.

Marshall laughed. "Mr. Smooth. He swept you off your feet with the circus act, huh?"

Fran glanced away, wishing that she and Toby had a more sophisticated story. "Something like that."

"Have all your boyfriends been jugglers?" Marshall kidded.

"Um, actually, he's my first one," Fran admitted, knowing that this made her sound juvenile and wishing again that she had a different story.

"Really?" Marshall looked at her, his eyes ranging

over her whole body and then resting for a long moment on her face. "I'm surprised. A smart, beautiful girl like you?"

Fran's knees almost gave out at his words. "Well . . . ," she mumbled. "The high-school dating scene can be kind of a drag."

"It wasn't *that* long ago for me. I remember."

Fran had vowed to stick to impersonal subjects, but now that he'd started it, she was pretty curious about a few things herself. "You know that girl who sometimes paints next to you?" Fran asked him. "Audrey?"

"Guess she couldn't make it tonight."

"Are you two . . . do you know each other very well?"

Marshall smiled, apparently amused by this transparent question. "You mean, are we getting it on?"

Certain that her cheeks were now the color of a fire engine, Fran nodded slightly.

"Nah. We talk when the model's on break, that's all. You know, like you and I are doing right now."

"Like you and I" . . . *Marshall put me in the same category as Audrey,* Fran thought. *So he doesn't think of me as some kid.* Not only that, Marshall and Audrey weren't dating! "Oh," Fran said, trying to sound as nonchalant as possible. Still, a smile crept across her face.

"My schedule's pretty full this summer, what with the job and my own art," Marshall went on. "Not a whole lot of time for anything else."

The implication seemed clear to Fran. *He*

doesn't have a girlfriend! she thought. She didn't know why she was so glad. It didn't have anything to do with her—she wasn't free.

But she *was* glad. No denying that. "All work and no play makes Marshall a dull boy," she teased as they walked back up the steps to the museum.

"So save me from being dull, Fran." Marshall gave her another one of those long, meaningful glances. "Inspire me."

Fran stared back at him, dumbfounded. "In-Inspire you?" she stammered.

"You know, inside. In class. Let's both really get into it tonight."

"Okay," Fran said. She was having trouble breathing. "Let's."

Back at her easel, Fran kept stealing glances at Marshall, and every time she did she caught him looking at her too. He'd smile and she'd smile, then they'd both turn back to their drawings.

Not that Fran could see the paper in front of her, much less the male model a few yards away. All she was aware of, all she could see, was Marshall. They'd broken new ground that night—they were forging an independent friendship—and all of a sudden just about everything and everyone else, including Toby, seemed irrelevant.

Her fantasy machine was going again, full blast. Fran tried to put the brakes on it, but it was hopeless.

I'm in trouble, she realized, feeling both elated and horrible at the same time. *Big trouble.*

*   *   *

"Last night I broke every single resolution I'd made," Fran confessed to Caley the next day.

Caley and Fran had met at the museum at lunchtime and were presently browsing the accessories department at Marshall Field's. Fran had spent the morning sketching and pining over the absence of Marshall, whom she didn't run into until she was on her way out with Caley. At least she'd gotten a chance to introduce Caley to Marshall. Now her best friend could finally fully relate to her dilemma.

"Which resolutions?" Caley asked, trying on a pair of sunglasses.

Fran ticked the crimes off on her fingers. "No daydreaming, no talking about personal stuff, no flirting."

Caley reached for a different pair of glasses. "You flirted?"

Fran nodded miserably. "I knew I shouldn't, but I couldn't help it."

"Fran." Caley shook her head. "Fran, Fran, Fran."

"I know." Fran grabbed a pair of sunglasses herself—she needed some dark lenses to hide behind. "But here's the thing. I'm pretty sure he doesn't have a girlfriend. He's not going out with Audrey from drawing class anyway. And he's only three years older than me, and when we talk, he doesn't make me feel like I'm younger. So I know I shouldn't, but I keep picturing us as a . . ." Fran gulped, then said the word. "A couple."

"Stop right there," Caley commanded as they shifted over to belts and scarves. "Seriously, Fran. I mean, I've seen Museum Guy—I mean, Marshall—now, and yeah, I agree, he's hot. But stick to Toby. You've got a good thing going there. A *really* good thing—you're in love with the guy—and that doesn't come along often."

Fran frowned at the belt Caley was modeling for her. "But that's the problem. Maybe I'm not in love with Toby. I mean, I thought I was. . . . I guess I am," she added.

"You don't sound too sure."

"I'm not," Fran confessed. "If I have feelings like this for Marshall, then I must not be in love with Toby. Right?"

"I don't know, Franny," Caley admitted. "I'm stumped. This is new territory for me."

"For me too." Fran sighed. "And man, I wish I hadn't ended up here."

They walked out of the department store without buying anything. Caley still had twenty minutes left in her lunch hour, so she walked Fran back to the Art Institute.

"What are you going to do?" Caley asked as they neared the museum steps.

"I wish I knew," Fran said. "I wish I could go back in time, to before I met him and found out that he was Toby's brother. I was having better luck forgetting about him back then." She chewed on her fingernail. "I guess I just have to try to stop thinking about him. That's the right thing to do, isn't it?" she asked, putting the question as much to herself as to Caley.

"No way," Caley said.

"What?" Fran turned to glance at her friend. "You have a better idea?"

"Look," Caley said, staring straight ahead.

Fran followed Caley's wide-eyed gaze. There was a couple at the top of the stairs—a guy and a girl, their arms wrapped around each other. It was hard to see their faces because they were in a total lip lock, but the girl had long auburn hair and a very short skirt. The guy had golden hair and muscular arms and was wearing a dress shirt, tie, and khakis.

The girl wasn't anyone Fran recognized. But the guy . . .

Her mouth fell open. Instead of its usual handsprings, her heart gave a sickening lurch, then momentarily stopped altogether.

The guy was Marshall.

Eleven

"I SAW MARSHALL with a girl the other day," Fran told Toby on Thursday night. She hadn't seen Marshall since Tuesday afternoon, but she'd been burning with curiosity ever since.

They were sitting on beach towels at the lake. "Must've been Calista," Toby said, his eyes closed and his face to the sun.

"Calista?" Fran repeated.

"Marshall's girlfriend."

Marshall's girlfriend. The two most unwelcome words in the English language. Not that Calista sounded like an English word. "What kind of name is that?"

"Greek or something. But I think she's Irish. I mean, of Irish descent. She goes to Michigan with Marsh."

"Oh." Fran felt limp and lifeless. "Have they been going out long?"

"All last year at school. Seems like one of those on-again, off-again things. Not that he tells me anything."

"So, is it off or on?"

"Well, she showed up the other day—her family's from Farmington Hills, outside Detroit—and he's been playing hooky from work to be with her ever since. So I guess it's on."

Fran couldn't help it. Her face fell. *Not that I should be surprised,* she thought. That was a pretty passionate kiss she had witnessed. *And not that I should care. It's none of my business. But . . .*

Toby shifted positions, resting his weight on one elbow so that he could look at her. "Why all the questions about Marsh?"

"No reason," Fran said, a little too quickly. "I'm just curious, since he's your brother. It's nice that he and Calista are back together."

"I guess." Toby reached over to flick a fly off Fran's bare leg. "I've only met her once. She seemed okay."

Fran swallowed. "Is she pretty?"

"Of course." Toby laughed. "We're talking about Marshall here. Appearances mean pretty much everything to him."

"Oh." Fran lay back on her towel, pretending to sunbathe. It was safer than talking. If she talked, she'd ask more questions about Marshall's love life, and at some point Toby would definitely start to wonder why she was so incredibly interested.

Inside, though, Fran continued to mull over this latest development. *Calista,* she mused, more than a little jealous. *The girl in Marshall's life would turn out to have a glamorous, exotic name like that. Why didn't I figure there had to be a Calista?* And now that she thought back to her conversation with Marshall the other night, she realized he hadn't come right out and said he was single. She'd just jumped to that conclusion. It had obviously been wishful thinking.

Fran rolled onto her stomach, resting her chin on her folded arms. Sneaking a look at Toby, she saw the silver lining in the cloud.

It was definitely for the best that Marshall wasn't available. It had been starting to look as though her crush was just going to keep getting worse. But knowing about Calista would change that, and if her crush disappeared, she'd be able to give all her attention to Toby again, the way he deserved.

"Are you free tomorrow afternoon?" Toby asked.

"Hmmm?" Fran snapped out of her reverie. "Uh, yeah. I think so. Next Friday I'm going to Wisconsin, but tomorrow I'm just hanging out." Her father and Emma had rented a cabin for the family up on Lake Superior. A nightmare in the making, Fran was convinced. Stuck in the middle of nowhere with Drea, the twins, and billions of mosquitoes. "Why, what's up?"

"I'm meeting this guy, Kyle, at Cabrini Green," Toby explained. "He's my counterpart for the out-reach program, and he wants me to meet some of the kids. They sound great. Most of them are in ju-nior high, so it'll be a big-brother/big-sister kind of thing. What do you say?" He gave Fran one of his sweetest smiles. "Will you come with me?"

Giving Toby lots of attention was one thing; this outreach stuff was another. Fran approved of it in theory, but she simply couldn't see herself as a volunteer, and she felt a flicker of annoyance that Toby had brought it up again. "I don't have time," she said. "I've got this job for Professor Baird and—"

"I thought you said that was getting boring."

She had said that. It *was* getting boring. "I'm still committed to him for the summer."

"The volunteer stuff won't really get rolling until fall," Toby persisted. "Come on, Fran. I promise it'll be fun."

Fun? Fran tried to see it that way, to see it through Toby's eyes, but she couldn't. To her it just sounded scary. Going to an inner-city housing project where there were gangs and guns and trying to bond with some kid Drea's age with whom she truly had zero in common?

"I wouldn't be good at it, Toby."

He looked at her, still hopeful. "How do you know?"

"I just know. I'm not a people person like you. I'm too quiet. Plus I already have a new sister, and I'm not doing so great with her."

Toby appeared thoughtful for a minute, his eyes still fixed on her face. Then he asked, "You know what I think?"

Fran dug her toes into the sand. "What?"

"I think you sell yourself short. Maybe you're

not a rowdy party-animal type, but it seems like you sometimes hide behind the quiet-girl stuff. You never put yourself out on a limb."

Fran stiffened, feeling hurt and defensive. "Are you ragging on me just because I don't want to volunteer for your outreach program?"

"No. *No.*" Toby shook his head vehemently. "I didn't mean to rag on you. It came out wrong." He placed his hand on her arm. "Hey. I really didn't mean to criticize. I think you're wonderful, Fran. I wouldn't change a thing about you."

Fran drew in a deep, shaky breath. Should she try to explain to Toby why she'd taken his remarks so personally? *I do hide,* she thought. *I don't go out on a limb.* But there was a reason.

"When I was little," she said quietly, "I lost the center of my world—my mom. When something like that happens to you, you tend to put a lot of energy into protecting yourself."

They sat for a while in silence. Then Toby put an arm around her shoulders in a gesture that told Fran he understood. With that simple movement all of Fran's tension vanished.

"Let's lighten up and have a little fun," she suggested. "Ready for a swim?"

"Water's too cold," Toby said.

"Come on." Fran adopted the cajoling tone he'd taken with her earlier. "I promise it'll be fun."

Toby grinned. "Okay, Delaney. You asked for it."

They'd worn their bathing suits under their clothes, and now they stripped off their shorts and

T-shirts and sprinted, holding hands and yelling, into the lake. When they were thigh deep, the water slowed them down. Turning, Toby put both his arms around Fran's waist and pulled her close. "We've never kissed in the water," he said.

The lake was cold, but with his body pressed against hers, Fran felt warm. "Promise it'll be fun?" she asked.

"Or your money back," Toby said, then put his lips on hers.

Fran closed her eyes. As they kissed, the rest of the universe seemed to disappear. There was nothing but the feeling of Toby's body and mouth melding with hers.

When they drew apart, Toby pretended to faint back into the water. He came up spluttering. "Wowie zowie."

Fran splashed him, laughing. "You nerd."

He gave her a loopy grin. "I'm never going to be the same."

"You're right, you won't be when I'm done with you," she teased, putting her hands on his shoulders so she could dunk him.

After having such a serious talk, it felt good to mess around in the lake, and they stayed in until they were both covered with goose bumps. Then they dried off, and Toby walked Fran home.

"This was a great date," he said when they reached her house. "Low-budget but perfect. Don't you think?"

Fran considered it. What made a great date, anyhow?

Doing something fun. Being romantic, but also being comfortable together. Having a lot to talk about, but not feeling as though you had to agree about everything. *Forget the fantasy stuff,* Fran thought. *A great date is just being with someone you really care about, and who cares about you.*

"It was a great date," she agreed.

Toby reached out to touch her hair. "You sound surprised."

Fran blushed. "I didn't mean to."

"Well, it's okay." He shrugged. "I know I don't look like a movie star or anything. I'm probably not the kind of guy you used to dream about going out with."

"You're not," Fran acknowledged softly. "You're a thousand times more real."

They kissed one more time, then just stood for a long minute on her front porch with their arms around each other.

Fran squeezed her eyes shut. Marshall had a girl-friend, but even if he didn't, she knew she couldn't jeopardize what she had with Toby.

Don't forget how good this feels, she told her-self. *Don't forget.*

The next day Fran forged ahead with her Marshall-avoidance policy. It got put to the test right away—Marshall hailed her from the sidewalk as she was about to enter the museum.

"Hey, Fran," he called. "My first tour's not until ten. Want to go for coffee?"

Fran shook her head. "I've got an appointment. I'll catch up with you later." And before he could say anything else, she ducked through the door.

She pulled it off again later when Marshall, leading a tour, cornered her by her favorite Degas. He gestured in sign language, tapping the face of his watch with an index finger to ask her to meet him, and Fran answered the same way, tapping her own watch and shaking her head to indicate that she wouldn't be around later.

Drawing class was a little trickier, but by showing up fifteen minutes late, Fran made sure that someone else—Audrey, in fact—got the easel next to Marshall's. Then Fran studiously refused to glance in Marshall's direction. The only time she looked over at him was when she saw him leave class forty-five minutes early.

Maybe he has a date, Fran thought. She wasn't even bummed by this possibility. She continued drawing, her shoulders straight with satisfaction. *See? That wasn't so hard,* she congratulated herself. *Marshall's out of the picture. My crush is gone. I'm cured!*

Twelve

FRIDAY AT NOON Fran watched from the porch while her dad, Emma, and the twins loaded their gear into the Pontiac. She'd talked her dad into letting her skip the family weekend in Wisconsin, but now she had mixed feelings.

Drea appeared at the door, lugging an enormous duffel bag. "Going away for a month?" Fran joked.

Drea dropped the duffel on the porch floor with a thunk. "Do you think I overpacked?" she asked.

Fran had to smile. "Not at all. Never can tell what the weather'll be like up there."

With a sigh, Drea flopped down cross-legged next to her suitcase. "What's wrong?" Fran asked.

"Nothing," Drea said. "I'm missing my usual Saturday with my dad tomorrow, that's all. He couldn't reschedule for next weekend either." She flipped back her curly dark hair to look at Fran. "He's going away with some new girlfriend."

Drea sounded bummed, and she looked so small sitting next to her big, lumpy duffel bag that it made Fran feel as if she should try to cheer her up. "But Wisconsin will be fun," Fran said.

"I suppose." Drea stole another glance at Fran. "I wish you were going too."

"Yeah?" Fran mumbled, feeling guilty. "Well, it's nothing personal. I just have stuff to do at home."

"Sure." Drea got to her feet. "Well, so long," she said, her voice lonely-sounding.

"Bye."

Fran watched Drea drag the duffel bag to the waiting car. *Drea could use a big sister,* Fran reflected. A moment later she thought, startled, *That would be me, right?*

"Not too late to jump in the backseat," Max called, waving to Fran before stepping behind the wheel of the car.

Fran waved back. "See you on Sunday. Have a great trip."

The car chugged off. Fran felt a pang of regret. *I should be going with them,* she thought. *And I should have said something to Drea about her dad's new girlfriend. I know what it's like.*

It was too late, though. The car was gone.

Fran's regrets didn't last long. *A whole weekend by myself!* she thought an hour later, smiling at her reflection in her bedroom mirror. *I have my room all to myself again. I don't have to share it with anyone.* Her smile deepened. *Except maybe Toby.*

Not that she was planning to misbehave. She'd promised her father she'd obey the usual house rules and check in with her grandparents in the next town every day. But as soon as the Y day camp was over that afternoon, Toby booked it over to her house.

"This shouldn't be legal," he said to Fran as they flopped onto the family room couch with their arms around each other. "I mean, in broad daylight, you know?" He kissed her. "Can we stay in this position all weekend?"

She giggled. "What about the music festival tomorrow?"

When Fran had told Toby she was skipping Wisconsin, he'd gotten tickets to a music festival in the city on Saturday night. "Right, the festival." Toby grinned. "Maybe we can bring the couch."

They had a pretty good time making out, but when they took a break to microwave some leftover Chinese food, Fran noticed that Toby looked a little pale. "Do you feel all right?" she asked with a concerned frown.

Toby tipped his chin in the air and gingerly massaged his throat. "I'd like to say I'm feverish from desire for you, but to be honest, I feel lousy."

Fran got a thermometer from the medicine cabinet, and Toby took his temperature. It was 103 degrees.

"Wow. You're really sick!" she said anxiously. "You'd better get home to bed."

"Can't I go to bed here?" he begged with a weak smile.

"No way," she said. "Come on. I'll take you in Emma's car."

Fran drove Toby home. He dragged himself upstairs to his room, protesting the whole way that he didn't really feel all that bad, but by now his face was flushed with fever. While his mother rummaged in the medicine cabinet for aspirin, Toby gave Fran one last mournful smile. She blew him a kiss good-bye.

Driving home, something occurred to her. *I didn't even look for Marshall while I was over there,* Fran realized. *I didn't think about him once. I can't believe it. My crush is really gone!*

That was good news, at least. As for her romantic weekend with Toby, though, it wasn't getting off to the best start.

Fran called the Kalbhens' the next morning, but no one answered. She was so bummed about Toby's getting sick when she finally had the house to herself, she just packed up her stuff and headed to the Art Institute. She sketched for two hours, then took her brown-bag lunch outside, where she spotted Marshall and another tour guide, a grad student named Joel, doing the same thing.

"Hi," Fran said, waving at Marshall. "I'm glad I ran into you."

He walked over, smiling. "You are?"

Fran blushed. Even though she didn't officially have a crush on him anymore, Marshall apparently still had a powerful physiological effect on her. "I just wanted to ask about Toby," she explained. "Is he all right?"

Marshall didn't answer her question. Instead he gestured to a nearby park bench and said, "Have lunch with us."

Fran hesitated. *I do need to eat,* she reasoned, *and I need to find out about Toby. And Joel's here—kind of like a chaperon.* "Okay," she agreed.

Just as they were sitting down, Joel slapped his hand to his forehead. "Shoot!" he exclaimed. "Forgot I said I'd cover in the gift shop. Catch you two later."

"Later," Marshall said as Joel took off.

So much for our chaperon, Fran thought as she and Marshall opened their lunches.

"What were you saying before?" Marshall asked.

"Toby," Fran reminded him.

"Oh, right. Mom was taking him to the doctor when I left this morning. She thought it might be strep."

"Strep?" Fran winced. "I really hope not. We kind of have special plans tonight."

"Don't worry." Marshall slung one arm around her shoulders and gave her a brotherly squeeze. "He'll rally."

Even though it was a totally platonic and casual little hug, his touch sent major chills and thrills up Fran's spine. The instant he removed his arm, she quickly slid a few inches away from him on the bench.

"Toby told me your girlfriend was visiting," Fran said, figuring that this particular subject would help her to cool off. "Is she still in town? Or did she go home to Michigan?"

Marshall's lips curved into an amused smile.

"What did Toby have to say about Calista?"

She squirmed a little. "Just that you two are going out. I saw you together once," she added.

"Hmmm." Marshall looked away. "Yeah, well . . . Calista went home. We had a fight."

Fran put down her sandwich. "Really?"

Marshall sighed. "I don't know why it always happens like that with us. Things'll be good for a while, but it's like there's a bomb ticking. Eventually . . . *boom*." He shot a wistful glance at Fran. "But I don't want to bore you with this."

"That's okay." Fran was anything but bored. She was eager to hear every single detail. Turning sideways to face him, Fran added, "I mean, if you feel like talking about it."

"We have this pretty intense connection. You know, a physical thing," Marshall explained.

Fran nodded, trying not to think too hard about what it would be like to have an intense physical connection with Marshall.

"But emotionally it's another story," he went on. "She's a business major. Really practical about everything. Sometimes I feel like she doesn't respect my work or goals. Just because there's no profit motive in art, you know?"

Fran shook her head. Calista sounded clueless. "She shouldn't judge you by those standards."

"Maybe not, but she does." Marshall sighed again—from the depths of his soul, it seemed to Fran. "It's not like she means to put me down. She just doesn't understand what moves me."

"That must really hurt," Fran said softly. Without thinking, she put out a hand and lightly touched his arm.

Marshall stared into Fran's eyes. "Yeah. It does."

Her blood felt warmer in her veins. Fran moved her hand away fast.

Oops. She'd been doing a great job avoiding Marshall, but there she was, right back where she'd started. Feeling a little too close.

"You know what?" Fran crammed her lunch back in the bag and jumped to her feet. "I just remembered I have to, uh, catch the bus back to Evanston. To . . . put the garbage out. See you around, okay? I hope things work out with Calista."

"We'll see," Marshall said. "Hey, I'll tell Toby to call you."

Toby. Fran gulped down a large serving of guilt. She'd been so fixated by Marshall's romantic troubles, she'd completely forgotten about her sick boyfriend. "Thanks."

Fran ran to the bus stop, feeling as though she'd had a narrow escape. What was it about Marshall? The more she tried to pull away, the more she felt drawn to him. And the whole situation with Calista . . . *She obviously doesn't appreciate or deserve him. Whereas I—* Fran caught herself, but not quite in time. The thought was out there. *Whereas I would be a perfect girlfriend for Marshall.*

She couldn't deny it. Marshall still stirred feelings in her. The wrong kinds of feelings. And lots of them.

*　　　*　　　*

116

At two o'clock Fran's phone rang. It was Toby.

"Hi!" she said, her guilt causing her to sound a bit too eager. "Are you better?"

"Nope." Toby's voice was raspy and glum. "It's strep."

"Ouch."

"And I can't take you to the concert tonight," he told her. "I'm really bummed."

The concert was actually the farthest thing from Fran's mind at that point, but she didn't want to hurt Toby's feelings by saying so. "Me too."

"If you want to go anyhow—"

"No," she broke in. "It wouldn't be any fun without you. Give the tickets to one of your friends."

"That's the thing." Toby paused to cough for a few seconds. "My buds all have other plans tonight. I mentioned the concert to Marsh, though, and he said he might be interested."

"Cool." Then Fran frowned, remembering that Calista was back in Farmington Hills. Was Marshall already seeing somebody new? *That didn't take long!* "Is he taking a date?" she asked.

"Sorry, that's what I was trying to say. Marsh said he'd go with you—if you wanted. Then you wouldn't have to miss out. Here, wait a minute," Toby said. "Let me put him on."

It was really, really lucky that they were talking on the phone instead of in person, because Fran saw her reflection in her bedroom mirror go white, then bright red, then white again. When Marshall picked up the phone on the other end, Fran actually had to sit down.

"Hey, Fran?" Marshall said in his incredibly sexy, deep voice.

"Y-Yes?"

"Toby told me about the concert. Sounds like it could be fun. But I'll understand if you'd rather skip it."

"Um . . ." Fran moved the receiver aside slightly so that she could chomp on a fingernail. She was simultaneously thrilled (a date with Marshall!) and terrified (a date with Marshall!).

Not that it would really be a *date*. He was her boyfriend's brother, and technically, outside the realm of her most private fantasies, they were just friends. She might have been stubbornly obsessed with him, but he certainly wasn't obsessed with her. He was just trying to do his brother a favor. Still . . .

I should say no, Fran thought. *I can't trust myself. Say no, Fran.*

"Sure," she heard herself blurt out. "Let's not waste the tickets."

"Okay. I'll pick you up at seven," Marshall said.

"Great."

Toby got back on the phone, but Fran was now too preoccupied to string together coherent sentences. "Um . . . I should really go clean the house," she told him. "Talk to you later, okay?"

As soon as she hung up the phone, Fran gnawed at her fingernails like crazy.

"Oh, my God," she said aloud to the empty house. "I have a date with *him*."

Feeling queasy, she gulped hard. "My boyfriend's brother."

Thirteen

B Y THE TIME Marshall picked her up, Fran had talked herself out of worrying. *I'm in love with Toby,* she thought. *And I'm not going to flirt with Marshall tonight. Definitely not.*

Still, the outfit she picked—a crocheted cardigan over a flowered sundress with a low V neckline— could definitely have been called flirty. *Nothing wrong with wanting to look pretty,* Fran reasoned.

Then the doorbell rang, and there was Marshall. He was wearing baggy canvas shorts and a faded plaid shirt that was missing one of the top buttons so it hung kind of sideways, revealing a tantalizing glimpse of well-muscled chest and shoulder. "Hi there," he said with an easy smile.

God, Fran thought, *give me strength.* "Hi."

"Ready to go?"

Too ready. "Yeah."

They walked down the path to where Marshall's

vintage British convertible was parked at the curb. "Cool car," Fran commented.

"Looks can be deceiving," Marshall said as they climbed in. "It's a lemon. Breaks down all the time."

Fran settled into her seat, putting her seat belt on. Then she tried—unsuccessfully—not to feel excited as she buzzed down Lake Shore Drive in this hot car with this even hotter guy. Clamping a hand to her head to keep her hair from blowing all over the place, she shot a glance at Marshall's profile. He was so handsome and intense-looking, with his jaw slightly clenched and his hair whipping back, his eyes narrowed against the wind.

They parked the convertible in a garage and walked four blocks to the concert. Inside, they milled around with the crowd. It was a big, open space, and the first band had already started. "Want something to drink?" Marshall leaned in close to Fran, but he still had to shout to be heard over the noise. "I could probably get into the over-twenty-one section and score some beers."

It wasn't the most romantic proposition—Fran didn't drink—but Marshall's nearness was so exciting, she didn't dwell on his words. "No, thanks!" she shouted back. "Soda's fine."

They pushed their way to the all-ages bar and Marshall bought a couple of Cokes. "Let's check out the band," Fran suggested.

There was a reggae group playing, and the music was funky and fun. They danced for about half an hour. *Does he like the way I dance?* she wondered. *Is he comparing me to Calista?* Then she reminded herself that it didn't really matter. They were just friends.

Trying to keep that fact firmly in mind, Fran pictured Toby sitting at home on the couch, channel-surfing and nursing his strep throat. But just as soon as her boyfriend's image popped into her mind, it popped right out again. Her brain was too busy short-circuiting from the sight of Marshall moving his body just a foot or so away from hers.

Then he jerked his thumb in the direction of the door. "I need some air. Do you mind?"

She shook her head. "Air sounds good."

"Sorry," Marshall said as they hit the sidewalk. "I hope you weren't having too much fun."

"Why?" Fran asked. "Weren't you?"

"Not really," he admitted. "I mean, it was nice dancing with you and everything." Fran blushed, attempting not to get too excited about the compliment. "But I guess I'm a purist," he went on. "I really only like two types of music: classic rock and classic classical."

"I see." Fran laughed. "Well, if you knew you wouldn't like the music, why did you even want to come?"

Marshall shrugged. "Don't know. Felt like getting out of the house, I guess." He gave her a look that seemed to take in all of her: her long, loose hair, her very flushed face, her whole body down to her bare sandaled toes. Fran's heart rate skyrocketed. He shrugged again. "Felt like being with someone I can talk to."

Was Marshall implying that this wasn't just a charity date? That he'd actually prefer to just talk to her rather than listen to the music? This was Fran's dream come true! "Well, um, I wouldn't mind that much if we didn't go back to the concert," she told him.

"Cool," he said. "Then let's take a walk—if that's okay with you."

"It's okay with me," she answered mechanically, trying to keep all excitement and emotion out of her voice.

As they began to stroll past the upscale restaurants and yuppie pubs of Halsted Street, Fran felt as though she were absorbing the Saturday-night noise and lights and energy of the city right through her skin. Her blood positively fizzed with excitement. *Is this actually happening?* she wondered. *It seems too good to be true.*

"You know, I think I remember the first day I saw you," Marshall told her suddenly.

Oh, yeah, Fran thought, her stomach performing a circus act. *This is really happening.*

"You were sketching in the Impressionist gallery while I was leading a tour," he went on. "Degas's *Ballet at the Paris Opera*. Am I right?"

She was stunned. That moment had been life-changing for Fran, but it had never occurred to her that *she'd* made any impression on *him* way back then. "I—I think I remember that too. But if you were leading a tour, how could—"

"Hey, it's just a job." Marshall smiled his slow, sexy smile. "I have time to notice pretty girls, especially ones who also happen to be talented artists."

Fran was so astonished by this admission, she caught the toe of her sandal in a crack on the sidewalk and tripped.

Marshall put a hand on her arm to steady her. "You've got to tell me something, though," he said. "That day I saw you sketching from the Degas, enjoying its beauty . . . were you thinking about making a statement to society with your art?"

Fran shook her head, puzzled. "No."

"So you didn't feel like you needed a political agenda to make it all worthwhile?"

Fran looked at him in confusion. "Um, no."

"I'm just wondering what you and Toby have in common, that's all," Marshall said. "I mean, no offense. I hope I'm not getting into a sensitive area or anything. But he doesn't get your perspective on art, does he?"

Fran hesitated. It wasn't that Toby didn't get her perspective; she just knew he didn't share it. "We're different," she acknowledged. "I mean, I always knew that. But he's not necessarily wrong. Just because—"

"I think he's missing the whole point," Marshall cut in. "Art should be beautiful for its own sake. We're just here to create and recognize and appreciate beauty. Forget all the sociopolitical stuff."

He stared at her as he spoke, and Fran lost herself in his startling blue eyes. She forgot to be annoyed that Marshall had interrupted her; she forgot about trying to defend Toby; she basically forgot about everything except for the intense physical chemistry between her and Marshall.

And it's not all one-sided, she realized. *The way he's looking at me . . . he feels it too.*

Marshall stopped at an intersection. "The neighborhood gets a little dubious here," he said, putting a hand on Fran's back to turn her around.

For an instant before turning, Fran stared ahead into the lights of the Cabrini Green high-rises. *The projects,* she thought. A place she'd never been and never planned to go to, even though Toby had friends there—the people he was working with on his outreach program.

But Fran quickly forgot about Cabrini Green and Toby. Marshall's hand felt warm through the thin fabric of her dress. He kept his hand there for a few steps as they walked back up the block, but even after he dropped it, Fran still felt electrified. In the meantime Marshall had grown quiet. She stole a glance at him. He looked upset. "Is something wrong?" she asked.

Marshall hesitated, then said, "Yeah, actually. I was trying not to think about it because I didn't want to be a total downer tonight, but . . . Calista and I broke up today. For good."

"You're kidding!" Fran had to remember to be upset for him and not elated for herself. "That's awful!"

"Yeah. She called from Michigan right after I got home from the museum." Marshall gave Fran a pained smile. "Dumped me long distance."

Fran couldn't believe it. How could anyone in

her right mind dump a guy like Marshall? "I'm really sorry," she told him, even though she wasn't in the least.

"It's for the best." Marshall's usually smooth voice sounded a little raw. "Who needs a relationship that causes you so much grief?"

Fran could tell that Marshall was just trying to sound tough; he really seemed hurt. "Still, it must be hard when you've been close to somebody," she said gently.

"That's almost the worst part," Marshall said. "Now that it's over, I'm wondering, were we ever really that close? Did she ever really know me or care about me?"

Marshall sounded so sad, so disappointed. *It has to be horrible, realizing that you've been going out with the wrong person,* Fran thought.

A shudder of recognition passed through her body. *Isn't that basically what's been going on with Toby and me lately?*

"It got me thinking, anyhow," Marshall went on. "About why it didn't work and all that."

"Why didn't it?"

"We just weren't meant for each other. Calista's a great girl, but . . ." Marshall stopped walking. Fran stopped too, turning to look at him expectantly. "Well, maybe if she'd been a little more like you . . ."

Fran blinked. What did he mean by that?

Marshall didn't take his eyes from Fran's. "Do you know how it is when you catch a glimpse of something that just seems . . . perfect?" he asked, his voice low, velvety, irresistible. "And you want more than anything to grab hold of it even when you know you shouldn't?"

Fran nodded wordlessly.

He took a step toward her. "And you find yourself thinking, if only . . ."

Fran was overwhelmed by the emotion she saw in Marshall's eyes—the hurt, the longing. He'd never seemed so vulnerable . . . or so attractive.

Marshall brushed her arm lightly with his fingertips. Fran's body grew tense with anticipation. She knew she had one last chance to move away, but she didn't. She couldn't.

Instead of turning around, she moved closer. She looked up at Marshall, and he cupped her face gently in his hands. Their lips met.

As Marshall's mouth pressed onto hers, Fran was pretty sure she felt the sidewalk shudder under her feet. As the kiss deepened and he wrapped his arms around her body, the sidewalk rippled and rolled.

It was beyond a doubt the hottest kiss Fran had ever experienced. It left her breathless and shaking—and torn by conflicting emotions.

"Fran, I don't know what came over me," Marshall said, pulling away. "I swear I never meant to—"

"Me either," Fran gasped. "I'm really sorry. You're just sad tonight, and I shouldn't—"

"I got carried away. It won't happen again."

"Good, because if Toby ever found out . . ."

Even as they were apologizing, they fell into each other's arms again. The second time around, the kiss wasn't remotely innocent or accidental.

And it was even hotter than the first.

Overcome with guilt, Fran told Marshall she needed to go right home, so they cut their walk short and he drove her back to Evanston. They didn't talk much on the drive, but as he walked her up to her house, she started to have a different sort of regret, one that had nothing to do with Toby.

Marshall and I finally got together, Fran thought, still astonished by this fact. *Do I really want the evening to end so soon?*

She knew she should just shake his hand at the door and say good-bye. Instead, with her heart banging against her rib cage, she asked, "Do you— do you want to come in?"

"I don't trust myself," Marshall said with a small smile. "And you shouldn't trust me either. If I can't keep my hands off you on a crowded city street . . ."

Fran wondered if he realized that she didn't *want* him to keep his hands off her. He was right, though. They couldn't trust themselves—they'd proved that. "'Night, Marshall," she whispered.

"'Night, Fran."

Marshall bent his head, kissing her lightly on the cheek. Fran closed her eyes, savoring the lingering sweetness of this moment. Then she watched Marshall stride back to the convertible and drive off into the night.

Inside the house, Fran collapsed on the living room couch. Now that she was alone with her thoughts, she felt torn in two. "What did I do?" she groaned.

She knew exactly what she'd done: She'd gone out on a platonic date with her boyfriend's brother—with her boyfriend's knowledge and permission—and then she'd proceeded to make out with her boyfriend's brother in the middle of Chicago.

Fran stared into the shadows of the room. She'd never experienced such inner conflict before. She felt so guilty when she thought about Toby . . . but she was still on fire from Marshall's kisses.

Fran put her hands to her face. *What does this mean?* she wondered. It was one thing to have a troublesome crush on Marshall. A crush wasn't real; it was fantasy. But now fantasy had taken over. It was pushing her real-life romance with Toby aside.

But something must be wrong with our relationship, Fran decided, standing up. *Or why would I kiss somebody else?* "I must not love Toby as much as I thought I did," she said out loud. "As much as I should."

The conclusion made her ache with sadness.

Fran went upstairs to bed, but her muddled, dizzy thoughts kept her awake for hours. *Can I be in love with two people at the same time? Which guy do I love the most? What am I going to do?*

There was only one thing Fran knew for sure. Relationships were built on trust, and he didn't know it yet, but she'd let Toby down. Big time. She couldn't lie to him about this. Sooner or later she'd have to tell him the truth . . . no matter how much it hurt them both.

Fourteen

S UNDAY WAS ONE of the strangest days of Fran's life. The weather was drizzly and gray, but that wasn't the reason she didn't leave the house. When Caley called midmorning, Fran let the machine pick up. *She knows me too well,* Fran thought, listening to Caley's long, chatty message about her new crush at work, Rob, aka Copier Guy. *She'd get the whole story out of me in ten seconds flat, and I'm just not ready to talk about it.*

Toby didn't call, which wasn't surprising since he probably still felt crummy. But Fran *was* a little surprised that Marshall didn't call. She spent the morning lying on the family room couch, listening to classical CDs and wondering if Marshall was thinking about the previous night as much as she was. Did he feel the same agonizing combination of euphoria and guilt?

Then, as she toasted a bagel for lunch, a horrid

129

possibility occurred to her. *What if Marshall told Toby?* She stared at the bagel, watching it grow cold and unappetizing. She'd already decided that, for the sake of her conscience, she'd have to confess sooner or later, but what if Marshall had beaten her to the punch?

Around three o'clock the phone rang. Fran let the machine pick up. But when she heard Toby's voice she grabbed the receiver right away.

"Hi," she said breathlessly. "Hey, how's your throat?"

"Still pretty sore. I probably can't go out for another day or two."

Toby's tone was ordinary-sounding. *He doesn't know,* Fran thought, hugely relieved, but also feeling more like a criminal by the minute. "Well . . . I miss you," she said, her voice catching.

"I miss you too. Did you have fun last night?"

"Yes. You would've liked the concert," she told him, cringing from the guilt that now overwhelmed her.

"Marsh said the music was decent. Coming from him, that was high praise."

Toby sounded so good-humored, so normal. *He trusts both of us,* Fran thought. *How could we have done this to him?* "Yeah," she managed to choke out.

"Well, it kills my throat to talk. I'll call you in a day or two, okay?"

"Okay," she said.

"I love you, Fran."

A single tear spilled down Fran's cheek onto the

130

phone. Toby was her first love. How much was it going to hurt to destroy this relationship?

"I love you too, Toby," Fran whispered, wondering if it was the last time they'd say these words to each other.

The rest of the afternoon stretched out endlessly. Feeling anxious and lonely, Fran kicked around the empty house, playing loud music to keep the quiet from getting on her nerves. Finally she settled down in the kitchen and got busy throwing together a big welcome-home dinner for her family. Cooking helped to take her mind off things somewhat. And for minutes at a time she almost forgot that Marshall still hadn't called.

But after a while, as she chopped vegetables to make chili, Fran realized that trying to forget about Marshall and Toby wasn't the only thing motivating her. She was actually looking forward to seeing the whole gang again—even Drea. As much as she'd complained about it, she'd gradually gotten used to the manic activity of a six-person household. And with just her at home, the place felt weird. After hours of solitude, she wanted someone to hang out with and talk to.

At six Fran preheated the oven for cornbread and started making a salad. When she heard the front door bang open, she ran into the hall, wiping her hands on a dish towel. "Hi, you guys!" she greeted them.

Drea was the first through the door. "Thank

God," she said, dropping her duffel bag with a theatrical sigh. "Civilization!"

Emma laughed. Her nose was sunburned, and she looked incredibly relaxed. "Don't let Drea scare you with stories about no running water and electricity, Fran. We loved the cabin—I've already booked it for another weekend in the fall."

"No electricity?" Fran smiled sympathetically at Drea. "No running water?"

"Can you *imagine?*" Drea rolled her eyes. "I couldn't dry my hair. I couldn't wash my hair. The water was from this cistern thing and it was, like, colder than Lake Superior!"

"How'd you guys make out with no TV for two whole days?" Fran asked William and Douglas.

"It was awesome!" William exclaimed. "We caught fish, and Max showed us how to slice out their guts."

"Wow, Dad." Fran laughed, turning to her father. "Didn't know you were such an outdoorsman."

Max grinned. He looked tanned and happy too. "I didn't either."

They shared a noisy, cheerful meal, peppered with funny stories about Wisconsin. Fran mostly just listened, her thoughts drifting periodically to Toby and Marshall.

But after a while, everybody else's good mood rubbed off on her a little. She found herself smiling, laughing, and even forgetting about her inner conflict for most of dinner.

Still, once the meal was over and the table was cleared, everyone went to their respective rooms to unpack and relax, and Fran was left alone with her thoughts.

She could've gone upstairs to hang out with Drea, but she wasn't really in the mood to try to make conversation with an eleven-year-old.

No. She was in the mood to talk to a nineteen-year-old. A very specific nineteen-year-old—who wasn't calling, for some inexplicable reason.

Feeling sorry for herself, Fran retreated to her dad's library, closing the door and curling up with a tattered copy of Vasari's *The Lives of the Artists*. She couldn't focus on the book, though. All she could think about was Marshall and Toby and the stubbornly silent telephone on her father's desk.

Did I dream that kiss on Halsted Street? she wondered, suddenly feeling tired and sad. *Maybe it would be better if I had.*

Fran needed a distraction, but her job with Professor Baird didn't provide it. At his office the next day, she stood at the file cabinet putting away journal articles with boring, obscure titles.

"There must be a thousand of these," she grumbled to herself, "with people like Dad and Professor Baird writing more all the time. Who reads them? Who cares?"

After lunch Fran rode the bus into Chicago, her mood lifting the closer she got to the museum. *I'll see Marshall,* she anticipated, *and he'll sweep me into his arms and we'll talk about the future—our future. He'll help me figure it all out. I don't have to suffer through this alone.*

But she spent a full hour wandering around the museum without spotting Marshall anywhere. Her spirits plummeted yet again. Why wasn't he there? Maybe he was sick. Maybe he'd caught Toby's strep throat.

Then, without warning, Fran's emotions did an about-face, and she suddenly found herself missing Toby. She almost called him from the pay phone, but she was afraid he'd be able to tell right away that something was wrong. Eventually she sat down in front of *Ballet at the Paris Opera*, taking out her sketch pad and pencil. But she couldn't draw a single line.

Purely by accident, she ended up on the same bus with Caley heading home. "Hey, stranger," Caley called, smiling when she spotted her friend. She dropped into the seat next to Fran. "How was your weekend alone?"

Fran bit her lip. She didn't know if she was ready to talk about this yet. "It was okay. Toby got sick."

"That stinks," Caley said. "You had the house to yourself and everything!"

Fran just nodded, unable to say a word.

"Well, how was your day at the museum? Was Marshall there?"

Caley's question was perfectly innocent. She couldn't have expected that Fran would start sniffling. "What's wrong?" Caley asked. "Franny, what happened?"

"I'll tell you about it somewhere private," Fran said, wiping her eyes dry.

When they reached Evanston, they got off the bus and walked down a quiet residential street a few blocks from Caley's house. "Okay. Spill," Caley ordered.

Taking a deep breath, Fran told Caley all about Saturday night: going to the concert with Marshall, Marshall's breakup with Calista, the kiss on Halsted Street.

"Now I don't know what to do," Fran moaned, sniffling again. "I have to tell Toby, don't I?"

Caley shook her head. "Absolutely not. What he doesn't know won't hurt him."

"Isn't not telling as bad as lying?"

"If you tell Toby, what do you think'll happen?"

Fran felt sick as she envisioned the scene. "It'd be awful. We'd probably break up."

"Is that really what you want? What if the kiss with Marshall was just a fluke? He needed comforting, and you gave in to this crazy attraction. It might not mean more than that. Why ruin your relationship with Toby over it?"

Fran considered Caley's words. It was true that she didn't know exactly what the kiss with Marshall meant. But she knew it meant *something*. "It wasn't a fluke," she told Caley with certainty.

"Has he called you?" Caley asked. "Have you seen him since Saturday?"

Fran was forced to shake her head. This *did* worry her. "He hasn't called, and I can't call him at home because of Toby. But maybe he's just being discreet. For Marshall, this is even more awkward than it is for me."

"That's the whole problem," Caley said. "Toby and Marshall are brothers. Do you really think you and Marshall could end up having a relationship?"

Fran nodded as she remembered the kisses on Halsted Street. "Marshall is my dream guy, Caley. We finally connected. How can I not go for it with him?"

Caley heaved a big sigh. "I don't know, Fran."

When they said good-bye in front of Caley's house a couple of minutes later, they still weren't seeing eye to eye. "Stick with what you've got," Caley told her. "Toby's a really special guy, Franny."

"I know," she said, biting her lip. "But so is Marshall."

As Fran walked home alone she thought over Caley's advice. *She thinks I should go on with life as usual. But I can't just sit around and do nothing. I already changed everything by kissing Marshall.*

Fran knew she had to take some kind of action. She just wasn't sure what it would be.

Her chance came the next day. Toby called at breakfast. "I'm better," he announced. "Taking one more day off from camp, but I can see you."

"Oh," Fran said, unable to echo his enthusiasm. "Um, sure. I'll be at Professor Baird's this morning. Do you want to meet me for lunch?"

They planned to meet at the student center's snack bar at noon. Fran spent the next few hours agonizing about what to say to him. *Should I tell him about Marshall? I could say there was another guy, without naming names. . . . Then again, I don't even have to say that—I could break up with him without mentioning anybody else. Or should I just keep my mouth shut, like Caley told me to?*

She hadn't worked it all out by the time noon rolled around. As she walked to the student center she was leaning toward the last alternative. Keeping her mouth shut was definitely the easiest thing to do for the time being.

Then she saw Toby.

At the moment he was on his unicycle, caught up in a Frisbee game. He was joking around with the older guys he was playing with. *Making new friends everywhere he goes,* Fran thought with a pang. *Toby Kalbhen, Mr. Nice Guy.*

He was the most open, honest person she knew. Fran owed it to him to be at least partly honest back. *I have to just do it,* she decided. *I have to break up with him. He shouldn't have to waste his time dating someone who cheated on him.*

When Toby spotted Fran, he pedaled over. Hopping off the unicycle, he gave her a hug. "Boy, did I miss you!" he exclaimed.

She hugged him back with arms that felt rubbery and cold. "Me too."

"Wanna grab a bite to eat?"

"Actually . . ." She darted a hesitant look at him. "Do you mind if we just take a walk?"

"Sure." Toby wrinkled his forehead, studying her face. "Whatever you want. Is there something on your mind?"

Fran bit her lip. *Don't beat around the bush,* she

advised herself. *Just get it over with.* "There is," she admitted. "Toby, lately I've been thinking a lot about . . . us."

"Uh-oh." He smiled, but it wasn't a genuine smile. It was a forced one.

"It's not that I don't care about you," she said hurriedly. "You mean so much to me. But I'm worried that we don't have enough in common to make it work."

"Don't have enough in common?"

"Well, like . . ." Fran looked to the ground to collect her thoughts. "Like we have different tastes in just about everything. And I'm kind of private, and you're really open. And you have such a social consciousness. The whole arts outreach thing—"

"If that's what this is about, forget it," Toby said, his eyes serious. "You don't have to volunteer. I want you to be you, Fran. I would never want you to do something you're not comfortable with just to please me."

Fran stuck her hands into her shorts pockets, balling them into fists. He wasn't getting it. He was making this hard. "But Toby, don't you worry about it at all? Don't you think you'd be happier with a girl who was more like you?"

He lifted his eyebrows, frowning. "I'm in love with *you*, Fran." There was a tiny quaver in his voice. "Sure, we're different in a lot of ways—we've known that from the start. But isn't that what makes it fun? It would be boring to date somebody who was like my twin or something. You and I can

138

learn from each other. Help each other grow."

Fran wanted to argue with him some more, but she was at a complete loss for words. Nothing seemed clear to her.

Toby took both her hands in his. They stopped walking. "Fran," he said, his voice gruff with emotion, "don't scare me like this, okay?"

She looked into his eyes, a million conflicting thoughts zinging through her brain. *I didn't tell him about Marshall,* she thought. *We didn't break up. I haven't made any progress at all.* But would it have been progress to break up with Toby? "Okay," she agreed quietly.

Toby hesitated, then put his arms around her. The hug was a lot more tentative, and a lot more fearful, than the one with which he'd greeted her just a few minutes before. His lean body felt tense. *He's worried,* Fran thought.

And I'm miserable.

Fifteen

WEDNESDAY AFTER WORK, Fran and Caley went to the mall to check out the sales. Humming happily, Caley tried on dozens of summer dresses and shirts and pairs of shorts. But Fran just shuffled through the racks, listlessly reading price tags.

"When are you going to snap out of it?" Caley asked as she held a flowered jumper against her body and looked in a mirror. "It was a close call, but you guys didn't break up. I'd think you'd be psyched."

"I know," Fran said. "The thing is, I can't deal with my feelings for Toby right now. I need to find out what's going to happen with Marshall." She let out a shaky sigh. "And he still hasn't called me."

Caley stuck the jumper back on the rack and pulled out a pair of wide-legged pants. "How come?"

"How should I know?" Fran snapped. "That's the whole point." She had no idea why Marshall hadn't called her yet, or why she hadn't run across him at the museum. She was starting to feel annoyed as well as insecure. *I didn't imagine the sparks between us on Saturday night,* she thought, fingering a silky tank top. *And I know he felt them too. So why isn't he making a move?*

"Well, it seems pretty rude to me," Caley commented. She had a bunch of clothes draped over her arm, and Fran followed her to a dressing room. "He has to know you're totally on pins and needles waiting to hear from him. Maybe he went out of town or something."

Out of town? In all her wondering, that hadn't occurred to Fran. Why would Marshall go out of town?

Caley must have been asking herself the same question. Inside the dressing room, she shot Fran a speculative glance. "What was the name of that girlfriend from Michigan? The one he supposedly just broke up with?"

"Calista," Fran said, "and they didn't *supposedly* break up, they really did break up. For good, Marshall said."

Caley pulled off her T-shirt. "Hmmm."

"What do you mean, 'hmmm'?" Fran asked, even though she knew Caley's "hmmm" could be translated into "I doubt it."

Caley slipped on a V-necked top. "I'm not trying to make you panic or anything, but it just occurred to me that maybe Marshall went to see Calista. I mean, they broke up right before you two went out on Saturday, right? So he kissed you on the rebound. Aside from the whole Toby thing—which Marshall

141

might feel as bad about as you do—there could be things he and Calista still need to work out. That might explain why you haven't heard from him yet."

Luckily there was a chair in the dressing room, because Fran had to sit down. *Could Marshall really do that?* she wondered, a sick feeling in the pit of her stomach. *Kiss me like he meant it with his whole soul and then go back to Calista?* She felt even sicker when the answer came to her. Sure he could. Hadn't she kissed Marshall and then turned right around and told Toby she still loved him?

"Fran?" Caley asked, her voice low with worry.

Fran hadn't even noticed that she'd begun crying, but tears were now rolling swiftly down her face. "Sorry. God, I'm so pathetic," she whimpered.

Caley found a tissue in her purse and handed it to Fran. "Oh, Franny, I'm sorry. It's just a possibility. Probably a really remote one," she added in an upbeat tone. "Forget I even mentioned it, okay? You shouldn't be worrying so much. It'll all work out. I promise."

But Fran went on sniffling. It was starting to look as though she'd gotten herself into a lose-lose situation. *Will it really ever work out?* she wondered miserably. *When? How?*

"Fran, can I ask you a nosy question?"

Fran and Drea were watching TV in the family room on Thursday night. Fran had been in no mood for company, but her stepsister had followed her throughout the house. She simply couldn't get rid of her no matter where she went.

Now Fran pulled a throw pillow onto her lap and slumped lower on the couch. "'Nosy question,'" she mumbled. "Isn't that kind of redundant?"

Drea frowned. "I was only going to ask because I'm worried about you," she said in an offended tone.

Fran raised her eyebrows, surprised. "Worried about me?"

"Yeah. You seem really sad. I just wondered if you and Toby had broken up."

Fran's arms tightened around the throw pillow. "We didn't break up."

"But something's wrong between you?"

Fran shot a glance at Drea. Something *was* wrong, and Fran was aching to talk about it. *But I know Drea,* she thought. *And if I tell her, all of Evanston will know by dinnertime. Besides, she'll never stop pestering me for more details.*

"It's not really any of your business," Fran said.

For a second Drea's brown eyes flashed with indignation. She opened her mouth as if to argue. Then a different expression came over her face. It was as if some inner light had gone out. "I thought when your dad married my mom, you and I would get to be friends," she said in a small voice. "But it looks like we never will."

That wasn't a question, nosy or otherwise; Drea had made a simple statement. Fran didn't know what to say, and it didn't matter, because Drea stood up and left the room.

"Thank God," Fran said to herself when Drea was gone, but the words didn't reflect what she

143

was really feeling. Emptiness filled her. She hugged the pillow tightly, but it didn't help. She still felt completely alone.

Later that night Fran sat by herself in her room. She looked out the window at the evening light in the maple leaves, pondering her mixed-up love life.

It had been five days since her kiss with Marshall and she still hadn't heard from him. The suspense was unbearable. She'd asked herself the same questions over and over but still didn't have any answers. *How does he feel about me? Does he want to see me again or not? Do we have a future together? What's going on?*

Maybe Caley was right, Fran thought, biting her lip. *The kiss must not have meant as much to Marshall as it did to me.* Her stomach did a nauseating flip-flop. *Maybe he did go to see Calista and he's not planning to get in touch ever!*

"I'll die," she whispered to herself, fighting back the tears. "I'll just die."

Even though he was making her mad by leaving her dangling this way, Fran did want to see Marshall again—like crazy. But what about Toby? This was the truly weird part, Fran decided, pacing her room. She was glad that she and Toby hadn't broken up the other day, that he was still her boyfriend, and not just as some backup insurance-policy type of thing.

I care about him too, Fran thought, *even though we're different. We've always had fun despite that . . . because of that.* "I must have a split personality," she concluded with a mournful sigh. "That's all there is to it."

She was about to pick up the phone to call Toby—just to chat, and maybe hear a tidbit about Marshall—when it rang right under her hand. She grabbed the receiver fast, before anyone else in the house could. "Hello?"

"Fran? It's Marshall."

The familiar deep voice sent a whole parade of shivers marching double time down her spine. "Hi."

"Have you been thinking about Saturday night as much as I have?" he asked.

Marshall didn't exactly sound torn up about it. In fact, Fran could picture his casual smile on the other end of the line. "Yes," she admitted, suddenly feeling a lot less conflicted herself. *He is thinking about me, about us, about the kiss. He does care!* "I was wondering when I'd hear from you," she added, just the faintest hint of an accusation in her voice.

"I took a little trip," Marshall told her. "I'll be at the Art Institute tomorrow, though. Will I see you?"

Fran's heart soared. Finally they were going to see each other again! The prospect was so exciting, she neglected to ask him about the trip. "What time?"

"I have some tours in the afternoon—let's meet beforehand for lunch."

"At twelve, out front by the stone lions?"

"Twelve it is."

Fran cupped the phone close to her face. "I can't wait," she said softly.

"Me either. See you tomorrow."

"Bye."

After hanging up the phone, Fran danced giddily around the room. This didn't necessarily make things easier—Marshall was still in the picture, which meant she still had a dilemma. If and when she broke up with Toby, she'd hurt him terribly, and she'd be incredibly sad about it too. And, of course, it would hurt him a hundred times more if and when she turned around and began dating his brother.

But I'm going to see Marshall again, Fran thought, mentally counting the hours.

For that night at least, that was all she cared about.

Fran arrived at the Art Institute at ten minutes before twelve. She paced along the top step in front of the museum, her long skirt swirling around her bare legs. It took a heroic effort not to chew her fingernails to stubs.

Even if it feels like a biological imperative, I can't just throw myself into his arms, she thought, fiddling with the hem of her dusty-pink top. *We should talk first. I need a game plan. But what? Think, Fran. Think!*

She still hadn't decided what she wanted to say when she spotted Marshall striding along the sidewalk toward the museum. *Wow, wow, wow,* she thought. She'd daydreamed about him all summer long, but there was no doubt about it. In real life he was ten times more handsome, and twenty times more irresistible.

Marshall jogged up the steps. "Fran," he said,

looking her up and down and smiling. "You look gorgeous today."

He grasped her upper arms, pulling her toward him. Fran's body was ready to move in that direction—extremely ready. She wanted nothing more than to feel Marshall's lips on hers. But she knew if they didn't talk now, *before* they kissed, she'd never collect her wits enough to have a sensible conversation. And there were things they absolutely needed to talk about. She had so many questions.

"Marshall, wait," she said, stepping away from him.

He pretended to look hurt. "No hello kiss? Guess I didn't perform well enough the other night."

Fran blushed. "It's not that. Believe me. But do you . . . have you been thinking about . . . us? I mean, the logistics?"

He crossed his arms over his chest, shaking his head. "Whoa, where'd *that* word come from? 'Logistics' doesn't sound very romantic."

"I know. But I am dating your brother," Fran said, a bit disappointed that he needed this explained to him. "In case you hadn't noticed."

"Haven't you blown him off yet?"

Fran flinched at his bluntness. "We had a . . . discussion. But we didn't actually break up, and there are still some things I'm not too sure about."

"The other night I got the impression you wanted to be with me," Marshall said, staring into her eyes.

Fran blushed some more. "Well, I do."

"Then what's the problem?"

"Toby." Her eyes darted to the ground to avoid

his intense gaze. It was a little too much to handle.

"What about Toby?"

Fran looked back up at him, baffled. Was he serious? Wasn't this obvious? She let out a frustrated sigh. "I'm worried that if you and I get involved, it'll really hurt him."

"*O-kay*," Marshall said, drawing the word out as if to imply that Fran's concern was silly. "But I still don't see what Toby has to do with us at this point." He shrugged. "I mean, if you're not comfortable cheating on him, just end things with him."

Fran swallowed, her eyebrows lifting as she digested this remark. How could Marshall think she'd be comfortable cheating on Toby or anybody? And how could he just dismiss Toby like that? "Don't you care about your brother's feelings?" she asked, unable to keep the edge out of her voice.

Marshall shook his head impatiently. "Toby can fend for himself. We need to go after what *we* want, Fran. Nothing else matters."

Fran stared at Marshall silently, shocked by his callousness. How could he be so coldly self-centered?

Other people's feelings do *matter*, Fran thought, her entire body stiffening. *Toby's feelings matter, and so do mine.* All of the conflicting emotions that had been building up inside Fran since Saturday night—all the anxiety, anticipation, excitement, and guilt—now expressed itself in a sudden burst of anger.

Had Marshall thought about her feelings at all when he waited five days to call? Or as he stood there right now, not even really listening to what she had to say?

"Trust me," Marshall told her. "Toby'll be fine. That kid always bounces back."

Fran still didn't speak. She winced at how Marshall referred to Toby as a "kid." And it was the other way around, she realized. Toby was the mature one. *Marshall* was downright childish. While Toby cared about the whole world, Marshall apparently cared about only one thing other than art: himself.

How could I have been so stupid? Fran wondered. *Why did it take me so long to figure this out?*

"Where were you the last couple of days?" she asked Marshall suddenly. "In Michigan with Calista?"

She knew immediately by the way Marshall's jaw dropped and his eyebrows arched in surprise that she'd hit her mark. "Uh . . . ," he mumbled.

Her anger now turned into rage. "So am I just a diversion? Are you planning to go back and forth between Calista and me, depending on what you're in the mood for?"

Marshall ran a hand through his hair, his eyes pleading. "Calista isn't the point here, Fran. Forget about her."

"I can't forget about her," she told him. Just minutes before, she'd been drawn to Marshall like a moth to a flame. Now she almost felt repelled. "But I do think we should forget about Saturday night."

"Come on, Fran." Marshall had regained his composure; the velvety seductiveness was back in his voice. "You can't ignore the chemistry between us. Don't you want to explore it?"

Chemistry . . . it *had* been there, to an unbelievable

149

degree. But now Fran wasn't tempted, and she was pretty sure she'd never be tempted by Marshall's charms again. "No," she said quietly.

"You can't be serious." He slipped an arm around her shoulders and tried to pull her close. Fran quickly wriggled free. "Fine," Marshall snapped. "But you won't get a second chance."

Marshall didn't look handsome anymore to Fran; he looked like a spoiled child who'd had a toy taken away from him. "Fine," Fran whispered.

Marshall took a half step in her direction, as if he were going to try with her one more time. Then, with a disgusted wave of his hand, he turned sharply on his heel and strode off.

Fran watched his broad back as he took one step, two steps, three . . .

This is it, she thought, her heart contracting painfully. *Are you really going to let the guy of your dreams walk away?*

Four steps, five, six . . .

Marshall was almost to the Art Institute door, but Fran didn't go after him. He hadn't lived up to her fantasies. He wasn't the person she'd hoped he'd be.

Fran couldn't face the museum that day, and maybe not again for a very long time. So she turned around to walk back down the stairs.

Then she stopped in her tracks.

Toby.

He was standing halfway up the staircase, a bouquet of roses in one hand. His blue-gray eyes were large in his pale, stunned face.

He saw us together, Fran realized, horrified.

She shot a desperate glance over her shoulder, but Marshall had already disappeared into the museum.

Toby was frozen in place. Slowly Fran walked down the steps to him, her legs feeling wobbly and unsteady. "H-How did you know where I was?" she stammered.

"I called your house—your dad told me. What's going on, Fran?" Toby asked hoarsely. "Are you and my brother . . . ?"

Fran wished she could lie—Marshall probably wouldn't have hesitated in this situation—but she couldn't. Not even to spare Toby's feelings.

"The other night, after the concert . . ." Fran licked her dry lips. "Something happened. We . . . kissed."

If possible, Toby's face grew even more colorless. "I can't believe this," he whispered.

Tears of shame filled Fran's eyes. In a rush she blurted out, "I'm so sorry, Toby—you can't know how sorry. I had a stupid crush on him—I always used to see him at the museum, and I just thought he was so cool. And then he seemed to be attracted to me too. But now I've realized that he's a—" She stopped herself before saying "jerk." "He's not the one for me," she said. "You're the one I'm in love with."

Toby stared at her. The hand holding the bouquet dropped to his side, the rose petals brushing the concrete step. "How can you say that? You love me, but you've been cheating on me with Marshall?"

It was exactly what she'd been wondering herself for the past few days. If she loved one guy, why had she kissed another? "Toby, you just have to believe me," Fran said desperately. "I made a mistake. God, I wish I could go back in time, but I can't."

Toby didn't seem to hear her. He was puzzling something out in his own head. "And you had a crush on him all along? The two of you made a pretty big fool out of me, huh? You must've laughed when I sent Marsh over to your house with those concert tickets!"

Stricken, Fran put out a hand to touch his arm. "I swear, it wasn't like that, Toby. I never—"

He shook her hand off. "My own *brother,* Fran. How could you guys do this to me?"

Toby's eyes brimmed with tears. Fran started crying too. "I don't know," she whispered.

"You tried to break up with me the other day, but I wouldn't let you. That's why I'm here—I wanted to make sure things were all right between us." Toby's voice cracked. "But you can have it your way now, Fran." Turning away from her, he jogged rapidly down the steps.

"Please, Toby," Fran called after him, not caring who heard her. "Don't go. Not like this."

Toby didn't turn around. When he got to the bottom of the steps, he stuffed the bouquet of roses in a trash can. Then he started running down the crowded sidewalk. Within seconds he'd disappeared.

Fran stood staring after him, her face streaked with tears. She'd lost the dream of perfect love she'd cherished all summer long, but far worse than that, she'd lost the one guy she truly cared about.

Toby was gone.

Sixteen

FRAN STILL FELT numb when she got home. She couldn't believe the events on the Art Institute steps had actually happened. And every time she pictured Toby's betrayed, heartbroken face, she started to cry again. *How could I have messed up like this?* she wondered. *Why wasn't I happy with a good thing?*

She was sure it must have been obvious to anyone with eyes that she was miserable. She figured it would take Drea only thirty seconds to start bugging her about it. Emma might take her aside and try to force a mother-daughter talk between them. Even her dad was sure to notice something was wrong.

But nobody said anything, even at dinner that night when Fran's eyes were still red-rimmed. Emma and Max were too busy discussing upcoming academic conferences, and the twins were arguing about who would get to watch what TV show after dinner, and whenever there was a break in the conversation, Drea started yapping about Bethany, her sailing instructor and current fashion and coolness idol.

Friday came and went, and Saturday too. On Sunday Fran slept in without meaning to and woke up to find the house empty except for a dashed-off note from Emma on the kitchen counter: *Off on an all-day bike ride. See you tonight.*

Fran crumpled the note and tossed it into the trash, plopping down into a chair. As she sat alone at the kitchen table, she listened to the silence of the deserted house. A few months earlier, quiet and privacy were things she'd hungered for like food. Now she had the solitude she'd craved, but it wasn't nearly as satisfying as she remembered it being.

Maybe it was because since that time, she'd fallen in love with Toby and then lost him. Toby had opened up the world to her in new ways, and without him she felt as if the walls had closed around her again. She couldn't believe how much she missed him, and couldn't believe that she'd wanted to break up with him to go out with Marshall, whom she didn't miss at all.

At midmorning Fran called Caley, but Mrs. Woods told her that Caley had just left to go in-line skating with Rob, the guy she liked from work.

Fran knew she had to do something before she went completely nuts. Getting on her bicycle, she rode aimlessly around the neighborhood. First she went toward the lake, but the minute she saw the beach, it reminded her of Toby: the day they'd met, that time they'd gone swimming, all their walks and talks and sandy kisses.

Turning back toward town, she considered riding to the art supply store, but then she'd have to pass by the pizza place where she and Toby had gone on their first date. Gulping back the tears, she looped around to her own street, dumped her bike on the front lawn, and shuffled into the house.

She flung herself onto the family room couch, and that brought on the most painful memory of all. *The day everybody left for Wisconsin,* Fran remembered, burying her face in the sofa. *Toby came over and we kissed all day. Then I went to the concert with Marshall . . . and that was the beginning of the end.*

She punched the cushion, helpless with grief and regret. "Will I ever get over him?" she whispered.

September arrived—the start of a new school year. On Fran's first day as a junior at Lakeview North, she was nervous because she was always nervous on the first day of anything. By the end of that week, though, she'd gotten into a groove. Science was fun, English was boring; her math teacher was cool, her French teacher was cooler; she'd been chosen art editor of the yearbook and was on the newspaper staff too. A few of her friends were even pressing her to run for student council.

"I'm too quiet," Fran said when Caley brought up the subject in the cafeteria one day. "Nobody knows who I am."

"Would you stop making it sound like it's a crime to be quiet?" Caley said. "A lot of people really like you, and everyone thinks you're smart. It's not like you have to be loud to be on the student council."

As she ate her pasta salad Fran found herself wondering what Toby might say about this. Something like, *You're selling yourself short again, Fran. Go for it. Show 'em your stuff.*

Maybe I should *run,* she thought, taking a sip of her juice. *It might be good to be frantically busy. I'd have less time to be lonely that way.*

One sunny Saturday she took the bus to the Art Institute. She hadn't been there in weeks, and seeing her favorite Impressionist paintings was like being reunited with old friends. But when she settled down with her sketch pad and charcoal pencil, she was uninspired. She doodled for a little while, then put her things back in her shoulder bag. *I'm tired of making the same old unoriginal sketches,* she realized. *I'm not learning anymore.*

On her way out of the museum she ran into Joel, the graduate student tour guide who was a friend of Marshall's. "Hi," Joel said. "Draw anything good today?"

Fran shook her head. "Wasn't in the right mood."

"Are you and Marsh still in touch?" Joel asked, walking out the door with her.

Fran flinched a little at the sound of his name even though she was way, way over him. The memory of the last time she'd seen him—which was also the last time she'd seen Toby—still stung. "No, not really. How about you?"

"Got a postcard from Ann Arbor the other day."

"So he's back at college?"

"And back with Calista," Joel revealed.

"I'm not surprised." Fran hadn't meant to sound bitter, but it came out that way anyhow.

Joel raised his eyebrows. "I hope I didn't say something I shouldn't have. You guys weren't dating or anything, were you?"

Fran thought about all the time and energy she'd spent crushing on Marshall, and their one night together. *One night and a couple of hot kisses,* she thought. What a high price she'd paid.

She managed a small smile for Joel. "No, don't worry. We weren't dating or anything."

At the bottom of the steps Joel grabbed a bus southbound to Hyde Park. Fran paused before heading to her own stop. Turning on her heel, she looked back up at the museum. It was really strange. All summer long, in Fran's eyes, the Art Institute had been about Marshall. Now he was gone, and his absence didn't make an impression on her. She didn't miss him. She missed someone else—so much it made her ache.

How come you never know how great something is until it's gone?

*   *   *

157

That Sunday morning Fran slept late. When she sat up, stretching, she noticed Drea kneeling on her own bed, looking out the window.

Fran heard a muffled sound. A bird? A squirrel? Then she realized it was coming from Drea. She was crying.

Fran hesitated, not sure what to do. Say something? Leave her alone? *Maybe Drea would feel embarrassed or mad if I butted in,* Fran thought. *Then again . . .*

She couldn't stand the sight of Drea's thin, shaking shoulders. It was too pathetic. "Drea, what's wrong?" Fran asked, crossing the room and sitting on the edge of her stepsister's bed.

Drea buried her face in her arms. "Nothing," she mumbled.

Fran put a hand on Drea's shoulder. "Obviously it's not nothing," she said gently. "Come on. You can tell me."

"It really isn't a big deal," Drea said with a loud sniffle. "Besides, it's none of your business."

Fran knew where she'd heard *that* one before. "Yes, it is," she persisted. "You're my sister, aren't you?"

Drea turned around to look at Fran. Her face was damp with tears; she looked painfully young. "I guess."

"I didn't see you at all yesterday." Fran had a sudden hunch. "You went to your dad's, right? Did something happen?"

"Something happened, all right," Drea confirmed, her voice cracking. "Dad has this new girlfriend, Jocelyn. Remember I told you about her?

Well, they're *engaged*. They're getting married! And she's only thirty!"

"That's not so bad." Fran gave Drea a playful pinch. "I have a stepmother too, and I kind of like her." As she said the words, Fran realized to her own surprise that it was true. She *did* like Emma, sometimes.

"You don't get it," Drea said. "Jocelyn's ten whole years younger than Dad. She'll want to have babies, right? Dad'll have a new family, and then he'll forget about me."

With that Drea burst into tears. This time Fran hesitated for only a second before wrapping her arms around Drea. "Maybe they will have kids, but your dad won't forget about you," Fran promised. "My father got some new stepkids when he married your mom, but he didn't forget about me, did he?"

"N-No."

Fran rested her chin on top of Drea's head. "Not that it's been easy sharing him with all of you. Being part of a new family was a big adjustment." *And I think I've finally adjusted,* Fran realized silently. "The thing to do is look for the positive side of Jocelyn. What's she like?"

"Actually . . ." Drea wiped her eyes on the sleeve of her nightgown. "She has great clothes."

They spent ten minutes analyzing Jocelyn's wardrobe, personality, and career prospects, finally deciding that she was so into her job, she wouldn't want to have kids right away anyhow.

"That buys you some time," Fran concluded.

Drea brightened. "And you know, I do like babies. William and Douglas I could live without, but I wouldn't mind having a little sister."

Fran smiled. "Little sisters aren't so bad."

Emma organized a family bike ride after breakfast. She didn't even mention it to Fran. *Because I always blow her off,* Fran thought as she strapped on her bike helmet. Well, as of right then, she didn't want to be left out.

"Hey, wait up!" she called to her stepmother.

Max, the twins, and Drea had already pedaled off. Emma paused at the curb and looked back toward the garage. "Are you coming along?" she asked, clearly surprised.

Fran hopped on her bike. "Yep."

A smile broke across Emma's face. "Well . . . fabulous!"

They headed north along Lake Michigan. The air was cool, but the September sunshine felt warm on Fran's shoulders. She and Emma rode two abreast on the bike path. "What a beautiful day," Fran said. "This is fun."

Emma gave her an amused glance. "That's why we do it just about every weekend."

Fran bit her lip. "You must think I'm a jerk for never coming with you."

Emma shifted gears on her bike. "Not at all."

Fran looked ahead. Her dad and Drea were in the lead, the twins right behind them. The sight seemed perfectly natural. *I've been the only one still holding back,* Fran thought.

She cleared her throat. "Emma, can I ask your advice?" she ventured.

"About what?"

"About, um, guys. You must be an expert, right?"

"Because I write literary criticism about romance novels?" Emma laughed. "Sure, why not?"

Fran told Emma about her breakup with Toby. She left out the part about kissing Marshall, but she did admit that it was her crush on Marshall that had gotten in the way of the relationship. "I still don't understand how I could've been so dense," she concluded, steering around a curve. "Why didn't I see what a jerk Marshall was sooner?"

"Well, I would've been suspicious of a guy who'd flirt with his brother's girlfriend," Emma said. "Right off the bat, that shows loyalty isn't high on his list of priorities. But I know what it's like to be blinded by someone's charm. My first husband was kind of a Marshall type."

Fran had never met Emma's ex-husband or thought much about him. "Really?" she asked, intrigued.

Emma nodded. "Brilliant, handsome, successful . . . sounds good on paper, but in reality he was so busy impressing the world, he didn't have a whole lot left over for me and the kids."

"Sounds like the exact opposite of my dad," Fran observed, watching him laugh with Drea up ahead.

"Mmm. The faculty party when I met your

father was the luckiest day of my life," Emma said.

Dad and Emma definitely had a happy ending, Fran thought as she took in her stepmother's smile. *Not me, though. There's no way Toby will ever take me back.*

"I totally blew it, didn't I?" she asked Emma glumly.

"Well, the romance genre has a fine tradition of second chances," Emma consoled her. "Think about Scarlett and Rhett, Elizabeth Bennett and Mr. Darcy . . ."

"Yeah, but I don't even have the guts to call him or write to him or anything," Fran murmured.

"Don't give up hope," Emma said. "What's meant to be will be."

They pedaled along in companionable silence, Fran thinking over Emma's words.

What's meant to be will be. It was a comforting philosophy, and Fran felt her spirits lift just a little. *Me and Toby, a second chance? Could it ever happen?*

A week and a half later Fran drove the Mazda to school because Emma had asked her to pick up Drea in the afternoon and drive her to some extracurricular activity. "Where are we going, anyhow?" Fran asked as Drea climbed into the passenger seat.

"Uh . . ." Drea pulled a wrinkled piece of paper out of her jeans pocket. Holding it at an angle so Fran couldn't read it, she gave Fran a sideways glance. "Lakeview South."

Lakeview South—Toby's school. Fran repressed a sigh. "What's going on there?"

"It's this new . . . club," Drea explained. "For girls from different schools around here."

"What kind of club?"

"A club to do, um, fashion design. You know, making clothes and having fashion shows and stuff."

Fran raised her eyebrows. "I didn't know you liked to sew."

"Sure I do."

Fifteen minutes later Fran pulled into the parking lot at Lakeview South. "You're getting a ride home, right?"

"I think so." Drea twirled one of her curls around her finger. "Will you walk in with me? I don't know my way around here."

Fran really didn't want to go inside. What if, on some off chance, she bumped into Toby? It would be horrible and awkward. She wasn't prepared for it. "I don't know this school either. There's bound to be kids around who can tell you where to go."

"I don't want to get lost," Drea said, her eyes wide and pleading.

Fran gave Drea a spare-me look.

"Please?" Drea begged.

With a put-upon sigh, Fran unbuckled her seat belt. "Okay."

They walked into the main lobby. Fran couldn't help but picture Toby hanging out there—talking and laughing with his friends, going to classes, getting books out of his locker. *Maybe he has another girlfriend by now,* she thought with a heartsick pang. A sweet, cute guy like Toby . . . it wouldn't take long for him to find someone new.

Drea pointed to the staircase. "The flyer says the meeting's in room two-twelve. You think that's upstairs?"

"Let's find out," Fran suggested, clomping up the stairs.

They wandered down a corridor. "Here it is," Fran told Drea once they were in front of the door. "I'm heading home. Call me if you get stranded."

She turned to leave, but something was holding her back. Or some*one,* rather.

Drea was dragging her by the arm into the room. "Come in for just a minute," Drea said.

"Drea, I am *not* joining a fashion club," Fran declared as her sister successfully tugged her inside. "I know we're getting along pretty well these days, but that doesn't mean I've developed the least bit of interest in—"

Fran's words died on her lips. A quick glance around the room told her that this wasn't a fashion club meeting. First of all, at least half the kids in the room were guys. And second . . .

The person sitting on the teacher's desk getting ready to start the meeting was Toby.

Fran shot an accusing look at her stepsister. "Drea!" she hissed. "How did you know about this?"

"Caley saw an announcement—she put me up to it," she quickly explained. "I'll hang out in the lobby for half an hour, okay?"

Drea ducked back into the hall, closing the door quickly behind her. Fran was left standing in room 212. Mortified, she looked back at Toby, who'd been chatting with some people and hadn't noticed her walk in. Now he glanced toward the door.

Toby looked stunned to see her—as shocked as she felt to see him. But for an instant Fran could've sworn he also looked glad. A light briefly bloomed in his eyes. Then the light faded and was replaced by a cold stare.

"Hi," Fran choked out.

"Hi, Fran," Toby replied in a neutral tone.

She had no choice now—she couldn't exactly rush out the door. Feeling embarrassed and nauseatingly uncertain, and resolving to kill both Drea and Caley later, Fran sat down in a back-row chair.

Toby glanced at the clock over the door. "Might as well get started," he said. He looked around the room, pointedly avoiding eye contact with Fran. "Thanks for showing up, everybody."

As Toby talked about Dreamscape, the name he'd given to the outreach program, Fran fidgeted with her jacket zipper to keep from chewing her nails as she stared at him.

She hadn't seen Toby in weeks, and his blond hair had gotten a little longer—it didn't stand straight up from his head anymore. His summer tan was fading, but his blue-gray eyes still jumped out of his face, full of life and warmth.

"Now let's hear from you," he was saying. "We'll go around the room and you can say something about why you're here. I should start, right? It's only fair. Okay, my name's Toby Kalbhen, and I'm a junior here. Some of you might know my cartoon strip from the school paper. I started this program because I've always felt that the more people you know, the richer your life will be."

Toby's eyes flickered briefly to Fran. Listening to him, looking at him, her whole body had grown tense with long-repressed emotion. It was all coming back to her: the way she and Toby used to talk, the way he'd shared his dreams with her and tried to make her part of them. *I always held back a little,* she thought. *The same way I did with my family. Even when our relationship was at its best, some part of me still held back.*

Toby's gaze moved on to someone else. "Anyway, I feel that somebody like me, who's lucky enough to go to this school and have all these resources, kind of owes it to the world to give something back. Not to preach or anything, but you guys must feel that way too, or you wouldn't be here." He gave an encouraging smile to a girl in the first row. "Your turn."

They went around the room. People had all sorts of talents; there was a drummer, a tap dancer, a potter, an actress, a poet. Fran was the last one to speak. "I'm Fran Delaney," she said quietly. Her eyes were on her hands, which were folded on top of the desk. "I like to draw and paint. And I'm here because . . ." Fran dared a quick glance at Toby— his gaze was expressionless and icy.

My sister trapped me into a face-to-face encounter

with my ex, even though I'm the last person on the planet he wants to see. "Because I've lived in a safe little shell for a long while, and it's time for me to see what else is out there." Fran lifted her gaze to Toby again. "Maybe Dreamscape will make me a better artist," she finished. "Maybe it will make me a better person."

Toby's eyes didn't look *quite* so cool and hard. "Thanks, Fran," he said.

When the meeting was over, Fran headed out into the hall with everyone else. She half hoped to hear Toby call after her, but he didn't. At the door she glanced over her shoulder. Toby had been watching her; when their eyes met, he looked away.

Fran walked down to the lobby. Drea was sitting on the floor doing her math homework. "Well?" she asked. "How'd it go?"

"Looks like I'm a Dreamscape volunteer," Fran answered, shrugging. She'd planned to chew out Drea and Caley, but now it didn't seem worth the trouble. What was done was done.

Drea stuffed her books into her backpack and stood up. "What about Toby? Are you guys going to be friends again?"

"I don't know," Fran said as she and Drea headed toward the exit. And she really didn't. There was plenty of ice to be melted between them. It was going to take a while.

If it ever happened.

Seventeen

Fran dreaded her first session with her Dreamscape sister, Maria, who was the same age as Drea. She was especially nervous about going to Cabrini Green, the housing project where Maria lived. But the moment she met Maria one Thursday after school, her anxiety disappeared. Maria was so friendly, so eager.

"Are you going to teach me to draw?" she asked, her brown eyes shining. "Do you have pencils and paper I can use? Here, let me show you some of my art!"

Maria's pictures were large, bold abstracts colored with markers on patched-together brown paper grocery bags. "I do have supplies you can use," Fran said. "And we'll work together on stuff, but I'm not necessarily going to teach you. You have a lot of ability. You'll be teaching yourself."

It was a warm Indian summer day, so Fran and

Maria walked to a nearby park, chatting as they went—Maria had a million curious questions. When they reached the park, Fran spread out a blanket and then took out two sketch pads and a box of pastel sticks. "I thought we'd start with these," she said. "I bet they'll be new for you, and they're still new for me. Maybe we can learn together."

They spent the next hour drawing. Since Maria liked abstract art, Fran suggested that they not attempt a landscape or a portrait—they should both just experiment. To her surprise, it turned out to be a good exercise. Maria worked with enthusiasm, and Fran did too. She got a completely different feeling than she did when she copied paintings at the Art Institute—freer, more original.

"Look at this!" Maria said, her voice filled with pride as she held up her sketch pad for Fran's inspection.

"You really know how to use color," Fran said with genuine admiration. "And this crosshatching stuff is cool."

Maria beamed. "I love pastels. I want to keep using them!"

They made a date for the following week—Fran wanted to take Maria to the Art Institute. Then Fran walked Maria home. "Thanks for coming over here," Maria said. "I know it's probably not someplace you'd normally hang out."

"No problem," Fran said, meaning it. "See you next week, okay?"

To her surprise, instead of answering, Maria

reached out and gave her a fast hug. Then she dashed off to her building.

Fran drove home humming to herself. She'd had ten times more fun with Maria than she'd thought possible. Considering the fact that she'd stumbled—or, rather, been pushed—into the Dreamscape program, it looked as though she might actually enjoy it. *Maybe I'll even be good at it,* she thought. *I wish Toby could have seen me!*

Fran smiled. She knew Toby would be pleased when she reported on her first meeting with Maria. Maybe it would even be the icebreaker they needed. *I'll call him as soon as I get home,* she decided.

When she got ready to dial Toby's number, though, Fran hesitated. It had been so long since she'd done this. What if he didn't want to talk to her? *But I'm calling on official business,* she reminded herself. *Sort of.*

She punched in the Kalbhens' number. The phone rang three times and she was about to hang up—she didn't want to leave a message—when someone answered. "Hello?" Toby's voice asked.

"Uh, Toby? It's Fran."

For a second he was silent. Then, warily, "Hi."

"I just wanted to tell you about Maria," Fran explained, trying to sound casual.

"You could've waited until the next meeting," he pointed out.

"I know, but . . ." She couldn't lie. She wanted something else from this phone call. Fran decided to take the plunge. "Toby, could we get together sometime? Just to talk? I feel like there are so many things we didn't get a chance to—"

"Sorry, Fran." His tone was curt. "I don't think that would be a good idea. I'll see you at the next Dreamscape meeting."

He hung up before she could respond.

Fran sat on the edge of her bed, her hands clutched together in her lap. She knew she shouldn't have had any expectations, but she couldn't help being crushed with disappointment.

She drew in a deep breath, willing herself not to cry. Aside from the phone call with Toby, this had been a great afternoon.

I'm not doing Dreamscape to try to get back together with Toby, Fran reminded herself. *It doesn't matter if he's impressed. What matters is how I feel about it.* And stretching herself—pushing out her boundaries, reaching beyond her own neighborhood—had felt good. Fran pulled out her portfolio, looking at the free-flowing, experimental pastel drawings she'd done when she was with Maria.

It felt *really* good.

When the next Dreamscape meeting wrapped up, Fran headed straight for the door of room 212. At the meeting before this one, she'd wondered the same foolish thing—would she hear Toby's voice behind her, calling her back? It hadn't happened yet, and after the previous week's phone call, she wasn't expecting it that day. Or ever.

"Hey, Fran. Could you stick around for a minute?"

Fran turned. "Sure," she said quickly, blushing.

Toby was a little flushed too. He waited until the rest of the group filed out of the room and then said, "I wanted to apologize for the other day on the phone. I practically hung up on you. That was really rude."

"It's all right," Fran said. "I guess I was out of line calling you like that."

He shook his head. "No, you weren't. I should've dealt with it better."

"Hey." Fran forced a laugh. "After what we've been through, you're entitled to some bad manners."

Toby didn't laugh along with her. "I wasn't trying to get back at you, Fran."

"I know."

They stood there awkwardly for a minute. Toby shifted his weight from one foot to another, looking at the blackboard; Fran crossed and uncrossed her arms, her own eyes roaming to the windows. Even though this encounter was weird, she was reluctant for it to end. "Well . . . ," she said.

"Well . . ." Toby cleared his throat. He was still looking at the blackboard. "Wanna go for a walk or something?"

Fran jumped at the offer. "Sure."

Once outside, they walked toward the retail section of town, a few blocks from Toby's school. Toby pointed to a music store. "How about looking at CDs?"

"All right," Fran agreed, relieved just to be talking to him.

They spent a couple of minutes browsing through music, still not really looking at each other. Toby was the first to speak again. "On the phone last week, you said you wanted to talk." His voice was stiff. "What about?"

"I guess about . . . what happened. That day at the museum." Fran felt the color climb up her throat to her cheeks. She leaned forward on the pretense of examining a CD, her hair hiding her face. "It was such an awful way for us to end. I hated feeling like I couldn't make you understand the situation at all."

"I understood a fair amount," Toby said. "I talked to Marsh."

Fran glanced at him. "You did?" She didn't know why she was surprised. Of course Toby and Marshall would've talked about it. They were brothers—they lived together.

"Yeah. First off, we had a huge brawl, that same night. But then, before he went back to Ann Arbor, we had a real heart-to-heart." Toby let out a short, uncomfortable laugh. "Well, I'm still not convinced Marsh *has* a heart, but whatever passes for one in his case. He was actually pretty sorry. I really don't think it occurred to him that he'd bum me out by chasing after you. He tends to just do whatever makes him feel good." Toby shook his head. "He'd cheated on Calista before, and she'd cheated on him, so I guess for him that's the way relationships work."

"I was the world's biggest idiot," Fran said grimly.

Toby shrugged. "Everyone makes mistakes. It's

173

over." He acted nonchalant, but there was the slightest quaver in his voice.

Fran stared at Toby. This was her opening. "I didn't want it to be over. That's what I tried to tell you at the museum that day. It took me a while to figure it out, but I wasn't in love with Marshall—I wasn't even in *like* with him. I'd completely romanticized him. He wasn't the person I thought he was."

"But neither was I, obviously," Toby said bitterly.

Fran shook her head. "No, to be honest, you weren't. You were kinder," she explained. "Deeper."

"Yeah, well, you know what they say." Toby's tone was tinged with sarcasm. "Nice guys finish last."

"Not always."

For a moment Toby's tough expression softened. There was a sad longing in his eyes. But then he abruptly turned his back on the CD display—and on Fran. "Well, I'm glad we had this talk. Don't think I'll buy anything today, though. I've got to run—keep me posted on how it's going with Maria."

"Toby, can't we please—"

"I need more time, Fran."

With that, Toby strode out of the music store. Fran watched him leave, not knowing whether to feel depressed or optimistic. *Is that what you call getting closure?* she wondered. *Was that the end? Or was it just the end of the beginning?*

That night Max took Fran out for a father-daughter dinner at their favorite Italian restaurant. "This is fun, Dad," Fran said as she unfolded her napkin. "But I'm adjusting better to the whole stepfamily thing. You didn't have to do this."

"It's not just for you, you know," Max said. "I enjoy having some time alone with you."

Fran suddenly felt teary, as she had all afternoon ever since her emotion-charged encounter with Toby. "I do wish sometimes that it was just us two," she confessed. "Even though I know that's as dumb a wish as the one I used to have when I was little—that Mom hadn't died."

"I wished that for a long time too," Max said. "It's not a dumb wish."

"Sure it was," Fran said bitterly. "It could never come true."

"I guess I disagree. I think any wish that expresses some need in your soul is okay. You don't have to actually believe it will happen."

Fran contemplated her wish to get back together with Toby. Pretty pointless and sentimental, if you asked her. "Well, anyway," she said, opening her menu, "are you going to order pasta tonight?"

Max was studying his daughter. "You know how much I love you, don't you, Franny?"

"*Dad,*" Fran said, a little embarrassed. "Do you have to get mushy in public?"

"I love you tons," Max went on, squeezing her hand. "As much as I ever did. Getting married again didn't change that."

Deep down in her heart, Fran knew that. But it felt good to hear him say the words aloud.

"My relationship with you will always be as

important to me as it was before," Max assured her. "But as for the rest of it, I wouldn't go back to the old days for anything. This'll probably sound corny, but I started living fully again when I met Emma."

Fran rolled her eyes. "It does sound corny, Dad."

Max grinned. "Okay, I won't elaborate. My point is that I think being happy with Emma is making me a better person all around. A better teacher, a better scholar, maybe even a better father."

The waiter came, and they ordered dinner. Fran thought about what her father had said. It was kind of bizarre to compare herself to her dad in the romance department, but the way he talked about Emma reminded Fran a little of how she'd felt when she was going out with Toby.

"Dad," Fran said out of the blue, "what makes somebody a great artist?"

Max chuckled. "Do you have a semester or two? I could teach a whole course on that."

"Summarize it," she said, leaning her elbows on the table. "I really want to know."

"A great artist is someone who breaks new ground. Whose works are one of a kind. Most artists' early stuff is derivative, copycat art-school exercises. Important artists move beyond that and invent unique forms of self-expression."

Fran nodded. "I used to think I only had to be good at drawing," she said. "I wanted every line, every color choice to be perfect and exact."

"Technique's important, don't get me wrong,"

her father said. "But it's not worth much without some heart and soul behind it."

The waiter brought their meals. "I probably won't be going to the Art Institute quite as often, Dad," Fran said, twirling some linguine onto her fork. "I think I'm done with all that copying."

"Maybe you're ready for something else," he agreed. "You have talent, Franny. See where it takes you."

See where it takes me. . . . It was scary, but also exciting, Fran decided. Because she really didn't know. There was no security, no sure thing. Just an adventure.

It was a mild Saturday in early October. Fran rode her bike out to the lake with her portable easel and stool.

She set up her easel a few yards from the bike path, taped up a piece of drawing paper, and opened up her box of pastels. There was a girl throwing a stick for her dog, and Fran concentrated on these figures rather than the lake or the sky, placing them in the middle of her drawing. She sketched rapidly in a loose, expressionistic fashion, with lots of color and movement.

After twenty minutes or so, the girl and her dog left. Fran stepped back to study her drawing. *I'll just keep working up the color,* she thought. *Make that the focus. Leave the figures kind of fuzzy.*

"Interesting picture," someone behind her observed.

Fran turned. There was a guy on the bike path. A guy on a unicycle. A guy on a unicycle *juggling*.

This time Toby didn't lose his balance. The balls didn't go flying. He pedaled forward a few inches, back a few inches, then pocketed the balls and hopped off cleanly.

Fran smiled. "You're ready to turn pro."

He grinned back. "Think so?"

The moment was surprisingly relaxed. Fran gestured to her easel. "Okay, what do you *really* think about it?"

"I like it," Toby said. "Honestly. Remember how frustrated you were by pastels before? You're definitely in charge now."

"I am," Fran said, nodding. "Maria really inspires me. I thought it was supposed to be the other way around, you know? But I seriously think I learn more from her than she does from me."

"That's so cool," Toby responded. "Exactly what I want the outreach program to be all about."

They stood for a minute without speaking. The breeze off the lake stirred Fran's hair and ruffled Toby's baggy cotton shirt. She felt happy just to look at him. The face she knew so well—the gray-blue eyes, the adorably crooked nose . . . "Toby," she said softly, "it's so good to see you."

"It's good to see you too," he said.

"Kind of a coincidence, huh? Like that very first time we talked."

He smiled sheepishly. "Not really. I stopped by your house first. Emma told me you might be out here."

Fran felt a rush of joy. He'd *wanted* to see her. "Yeah?"

"Yeah."

"Well, your timing's pretty good," Fran told him. "I'm ready to take a break. Want to ride up the lake a ways?"

"Sure," Toby said. "I have a proposition for you, though."

"What is it?"

"You ride the unicycle."

Fran laughed. "Oh, no."

"Come on, Fran. Just try it."

She was about to refuse point-blank. Then she laughed again. What did she have to lose? "Okay, but if I fall off and break something, I plan to sue. My uncle's a lawyer."

"I'll keep that in mind." Toby steadied the unicycle while Fran climbed on.

"What do I do?" she asked nervously.

"Just pedal," he instructed. "Keep your eyes straight ahead and hold your arms out to the side for balance."

Fran stuck out her arms and burst out laughing. "I must look like an idiot!"

"Who cares?" he asked. "Okay, I'm going to give you a little push."

"Oh, God," Fran groaned, still laughing.

"Here goes."

She started pedaling. The unicycle wobbled. "Help!" she screeched, but kept pedaling anyway. "Hey, look! I'm doing it!"

"You are! You're doing it!" Toby cheered.

Suddenly the wheel twisted under her. Instinctively

Fran twisted her waist the other way, trying to recover her balance, but it was too late. The unicycle tilted, and she went flying—straight into Toby's arms.

He caught her, holding her close in order to set her back on her feet. "Congratulations," he said, smiling. "You're now officially a nut, just like me."

Toby's arms were still around her. Fran realized she was tingling from head to toe.

Still smiling, Toby pulled her closer and pressed his lips against her forehead.

Fran sighed happily. It was a familiar feeling, and she knew exactly what it meant. *I'm falling for this guy*, she thought. *Again*. And this time Fran knew it was for real. If Toby was willing to forgive her—and it seemed as though he was—she'd be sure never to let a foolish fantasy come between them again.

Toby was the only guy Fran was dreaming about now.

Do you ever wonder about falling in love? About members of the opposite sex? Do you need a little friendly advice but have no one to turn to? Well, that's where we come in . . . Jenny and Jake. Send us those questions you're dying to ask, and we'll give you the straight scoop on life and love.

DEAR JAKE

Q: *I just moved to a new neighborhood and made friends with a girl and her brother who live across the street. Steve and Kelly don't get along very well—they're always fighting, and I end up in the middle. To complicate things, Steve and I want to be more than just friends, but I don't want Kelly to get upset if I become involved with her brother. She already has a problem with Steve and me being friends, so I'm not sure how she'll react to us dating. I don't want to cause any more problems between the two of them, and I don't want to lose either friendship. What should I do?*

LK, Sarasota, FL

A: Sounds to me like your typical case of sibling rivalry. I'm sure this isn't the first time Steve and Kelly have fought for the attention of a friend, so I wouldn't blame yourself. If you're worried about Kelly's getting upset at the possibility of your dating her brother, make sure you talk to her about it first, girl to girl. Tell her how much you like her brother and that you want to spend more time with him. Let her know that you and she will still spend time together and that nothing will change that. You may also want to tell Kelly and Steve how uncomfortable it makes you when they put you in the middle of their fights.

DEAR JENNY

Q: *I dated a guy for a few months until he broke up with me for another girl. I loved him a lot, and even though he broke my heart, I still love him. The problem is it's been ten months since we broke up and I still feel the same way. What can I do to finally get over him or to get him interested in me again?*

SB, Crittenden, KY

A: I sympathize with you for having your heart broken, but ten months is a long time to spend getting over a relationship. Don't expend so much energy trying to figure out ways to get him interested in you again—that's energy you could be putting into something or someone more viable. What about getting back up on the horse? While it may be the furthest thing from your mind, dating is certainly better than pining away for your ex while trying to figure out ways to get him interested in you again. It can be a good way to get over a broken heart, and you may even have some fun! If your heart's not into dating just yet, why don't you try joining a club at school or picking up a hobby, something that will keep you busy and occupy some of your free time? You'll be amazed at how much better you'll feel once you put your mind on other things.

Do you have any questions about love? Although we can't respond individually to your letters, you just might find your questions answered in our column. Write to:

Jenny Burgess or Jake Korman
c/o 17th Street Productions,
a division of Daniel Weiss Associates, Inc.
33 West 17th Street
New York, NY 10011

Don't miss any of the books in *Love Stories* —the romantic series from Bantam Books!

SUPER EDITIONS